GREENWOOD COVE

Sunshine Walkingstick, Book 1

CELIA ROMAN

BONE DIGGERS PRESS
www.bonediggerspress.com

First edition © 2017 C.D. Watson. All Rights Reserved.
Cover design © Nocturne Art.
Published by Bone Diggers Press, Clayton, Georgia.
ISBN 978-1-943465-20-0

10 9 8 7 6 5 4 3 2

1

Was a pooka what got me into this business. Not an adorable one like the books lined along my walls claimed they was, when they was a-willing. This'un took my son, a sweet angel of a boy what never did nobody no harm, took him and God above knowed what it did to my baby.

We never found him, only the blood. Dear Lord, the blood.

I swallowed the bile down, nearly choking on the acid grating along my throat.

My sweet, sweet baby rested in Heaven now. I held on to that hope with ever thing in me. He weren't baptized like the Good Book said he orta be, but God's got a special place in his wide heart for young'uns. That's what the preacher man said leastwise, and if you can't believe a preacher man, who can you believe?

That pooka? I sent it straight to Ol' Scratch, quick as I could find it, with my heart all cold like the great sea of ice on top of the world. I followed it for three days, no food in my gut, nothing 'cept a hunting knife and a bottle of water to get me through. My daddy taught me that before he run off with that vacuum cleaner salesman. Not much else, but by golly, he taught me how to track.

My mama? She in prison now. Was her what taught me how to kill. She sure done a number on my daddy. I never could look on her straight like again, not after seeing what she done to him. That didn't stop me none from doing the same to that pooka. You mess with my baby, you gonna pay.

I tucked my fingers into the place between my breasts what hurt something fierce ever time Henry come to mind, God rest his soul.

If the man sitting in front of me was thinking hard on how I killed a pooka with not much more'n my bare hands, assuming he knowed, it sure didn't show. His hard hazel eyes followed my fingers from the scarred top of what passed for a desk to the place where Henry lived, and lingered for a good long while on my skeeter bite sized breasts.

Weren't no never mind to me where his eyes rested, long as his hands didn't follow.

Lordy, them nimble hands. Long fingers, calloused palms. A tug of heat warmed me down low between my thighs. Mmm, what them hands could do to a woman. I heard the rumors. 'Course I had. Small town gossip run thick through the Georgia pine, and this man in particular was a favorite topic of the local women folk, him being who he was. Rumor had it Riley Treadwell knowed exactly what to do with them hands, where to put 'em, how to move 'em, and a whole lot more besides.

I shoved them thoughts away lickety split. Maybe if his long body was wrapped in something 'sides a worn t-shirt and jeans cupping him in places a woman wanted to know best, them thoughts wouldn'ta been running around in my noggin.

I rapped my knuckles hard on the wooden plank of my desk, grabbing his attention before he got any notions about my breasts. Or worse, before I got any notions about what was under them jeans of his.

"What you want, Riley?" I asked. "I ain't got all day."

Riley slid a finger along firm lips over the beginnings of a smile, probably from being caught ogling me like a teenager just figuring out where God intended his pecker to go. Them hazel eyes sparkled a little, but they raised up 'til they met mine. "A friend of mine has a problem."

I let my eyes go hard as his, what good it'd do. Riley was about a foot taller'n me and wide as a full grown oak. On top of that, he was a lawman descended from a long line of lawmen. Me, I was half as big as a cricket and twice as skinny, and the only kin I had to the law was when my family stepped chin deep into the wrong side of it. I was David to Riley's Goliath, only a lot less scary looking than the shepherd boy ever thought on being, even with my mama's coon crazy eyes staring out at the world.

"I don't work with no intermediaries," I said. "You tell your *friend* to get his lazy butt out here if he wants my help."

Riley's rough bark of laughter shivered down my spine, halfway between honey and hell. "*She* couldn't even get up your driveway. You ever think about grading it once in a while?"

She, huh? A stone cold knot fixed itself in my gut. Weren't jealousy, couldn't be. Riley Treadwell and me didn't even live on the same planet, far as man-woman relations went. I was *beneath his notice*, something I learnt the hard way back in high school, somewhat before I lost what sense God give me and let that fool Terry Whitehead plant Henry in my belly.

"You ever think on minding your own beeswax?"

"Jesus, Sunny. I'm trying to bring you a paying client."

"If *she* can't get up the drive, *she* don't need no help, do she?" I snapped. "And don't take the Lord's name in vain."

His firm lips twisted into something akin to a smirk. "You're telling me not to cuss? That's rich, darlin'."

"I got right with Jesus."

And I had, sorta, right along the time I learnt about Henry. I done the whole bit of Sunday School and church meetings and all that before that pooka took him into the deep wood between here and Fame's trailer. 'Course after that, me and Jesus ain't had two words to spit on each other. That weren't none of Riley's beeswax neither, though.

"I know your mama learnt you better," I said.

He rolled them hazel eyes toward the ceiling of my trailer. "Are you gonna help me or not?"

I was thinking *not*, right up 'til my mind lit on the coffee tin serving as my bank. Well, crud. Helping Riley weren't nothing I wanted no part of, but I liked to eat ever once in a while. The roll of green bills tucked away from the dribbles of honest work throwed my way was getting mighty thin. Weren't a lick of other business in sight neither 'cept some of Fame's, and I done shed myself of that line of work.

"What's the problem?" I asked, and tried to ignore the triumph in that smooth grin of his.

"There's something out on Lake Burton," he said, "tearing through dock pilings and doing a lot of damage."

I curled my upper lip into a sneer. "So the muckity mucks is losing some money on repair bills. What's it to me?"

"I don't think it's that simple, Sunny." A furrow appeared in Riley's brow and his eyes went all serious like, losing their brightness. "I dove down under Belinda's dock—"

The breath squeezed right outta my chest. "Belinda who?"

He hesitated long enough to tumble my heart into a sick nosedive. "Belinda Arrowood."

"You mean Belinda Heaton, your ex-girlfriend, head cheerleader, and all around bitch." I stood up, shoving my chair back against the wall as I did. *You're beneath his notice, sugar.* I put up with that crap back in high school. Didn't have to now. "Get out."

"Sunny, come on. That was a long time ago."

"Not so long as my memory."

I reached under my desk and pulled out the Ruger LCP .380 holstered there in case of emergencies sorta like the one I was in now. Didn't point it at him. Weren't no need to. Riley done his time, six years of hard labor under Uncle Sam's thumb in Afghanistan, dodging bullets raining down all around him. He knowed one end of a gun from the other, and he sure as tootin' knowed not to push Famous Carson's niece.

I jerked my chin at the door, case he weren't catching my drift. "Get on out, now."

He stood slowly, unfolding his long length as he stared me down, or tried to. Took a lot more'n him to make me blink. "That thing legal?"

I snorted. *As if.* "You ain't no lawman in my home, Riley Treadwell, not unless you got a warrant."

"Christ, Sunny. I'm with the DNR. That's hardly the kind of law you need to worry about unless you're hunting out of season or digging up wildflowers."

Well, reckon he hadn't found the Mary Jane my cousins planted in clusters 'long and along. Never on my property, no way, no how, but pretty much ever where else within a coupla miles' walk, including state parks and national forest. Riley finding that orta be fun to watch.

He sighed, though he didn't look a bit resigned. "Walk me out?"

"If you was invited, I'd walk you out. Come to that, if you was welcome, I wouldn't be handing you your hat."

"Ouch."

His mouth tilted into that smile again, the one he'd worn when I forced his eyes away from my teeniny breasts. Them eyes took on a glow, soft and hot and kinda delicious, truth be told. Riley'd been a handsome feller back in high school when his body was still kinda lean like and growing. Now, between his heavy muscles and flat abdomen and a crown of auburn hair nearly touching the sky, he'd filled out in a way what sent a sane woman's good sense flying right outta the nearest window.

Thankfully, I only had a passing acquaintance with sane.

He shifted into a wide-legged stance and crossed his arms over that fine, fine chest, and my breath went kinda shallow in my lungs. Lordy, if that's all it took to wet my whistle, I needed to get out more.

"I'm grilling out tonight," he said. "Thick steaks, baked sweet potatoes. Why don't you come over and we'll hammer out the line between guest and intruder?"

I blinked, then bit my tongue against the curse what popped into my mouth. I hadn't lost a staring contest with him since we was kids, dang his sorry hide. Now I was gonna have to put a quarter in the cussing jar, two if I counted using the word *bitch* to describe Riley's ex-girlfriend, which I didn't. Calling a spade a spade weren't on no level with cursing.

"I got plans," I said. "Thanks anyhow."

"You're a lot of things, Sunshine, but I never thought you were a liar."

He left without saying nothing else, didn't need to. I could about hear what he was thinking. Riley Treadwell would be back, and when he come, I'd have a sight more to worry on than taking a job for that nasty piece of work calling herself Belinda Arrowood.

WHEN THE DOOR closed on Riley, I dug a quarter outta my pocket and dropped it into the gallon-sized mason jar on the kitchen counter through the hole slit in the lid. It was half full already and I'd only been adding to it the last coupla months or so. Before that, I emptied the sucker into one of my daddy's old t-shirts, cut in two and tied together to hold the lot, and then I snuck out to the church and set the makeshift sack in front of the door for the preacher man to find. I figured I was beyond redemption myself, but that money might keep him working another day, saving souls for the

Lord and adding weight to Heaven's tally.

I filled a lot of them sacks in the past three years.

Since my gun was already out, I broke it down for a good, thorough cleaning right there on my desk while my mind rolled over Belinda's alleged problem.

Lake Burton's dam was finished back in 1919. Nearly soon as the thing went up, tall tales concerning the lake's murky depths sprung up amongst the locals, about whole buildings left under the water and a thick mess of other hogwash. Not a blessed soul took them tales serious, not even the cussed tourists clogging our roads day in and day out.

Wouldn't hurt to take a gander at the problem nohow, real subtle like. I didn't take the local paper, didn't rightly enjoy seeing my own kin's names in the police blotter week after week, but I knowed where I could get ahold of the past coupla issues.

And there was always Injun Bob's, if push come to shove and that worthless editor kept the good stuff out like she always done.

I finished cleaning my pistol, inserted the magazine, and chambered a round. Jacked the magazine out, loaded another round, popped the magazine back in. Hey, ever single bullet counts when you got monsters breathing down your neck.

I holstered the .380 under the desk and snickered as Riley's question floated through my head. Like any member of Fame Carson's family'd think about registering a firearm, let alone procuring one on Riley's side of the law. We was criminals, not stupid. Well, most of us wasn't stupid, not too much so, leastwise. I didn't count Gentry amongst that number. Bless his heart, he was a sweet boy and might've amounted to something if his mama hadn't done meth while she was carrying him. Fame kicked her out for it. Well, that and he caught her messing around on him with his no account brother. We ain't heard from her since, thank the Lord, and good riddance.

'Course, there was a better'n fair chance Fame'd wrung

her gizzard neck and buried her in the deep wood, but who was I to judge? A monster's a monster. Sometimes they was human to boot.

The front door rattled under somebody's fist. Weren't Riley. He was one to bide his time, line his ducks up in a row, and strike like a rattler, hard and fast and deadly, sure, but usually when you least expected it. Fame or one of his boys woulda walked on in. Might be business. Doubted it, though. That road really did need a good scraping.

"Come on in," I hollered, and weren't surprised none when Melissa Duggins poked her pretty head in. She was about the only family I had what respected my privacy.

About two years after Henry was born, being a decade or so after Fame run his wife off, Melissa showed up on my uncle's doorstep carrying a backpack, claiming to be a lost hiker. Weren't no stretch to believe it. Hikers went missing all the time 'round these parts. We done searched for our share, probably would again. Fame didn't want nobody stumbling on his extralegal enterprises for one, but for another, a body could die in the deep wood if he weren't real careful. Way Fame figured it, we was doing a neighborly deed by helping, kind of a tit for tat. Someday, one of us might be lost and need the extra eyes, though it weren't likely. We all knowed the deep wood like the back of our hands, even Gentry.

No, it weren't the claim what was suspect. Through hikers was skinny folk, lean from long months on the trail. Melissa's voluptuous body give her away. Fame took her in anyhow, ensnared by loneliness or her wide, violet eyes or the soft womanliness of her voice. Didn't matter none. She done right by him, feeding him and the boys up, taking care of us all, and made Fame happy as I ever seen him.

"Hey, Missy. Fame unchain you from the stove?"

She glided on bare feet across the worn puke green carpet I didn't have the money to replace and plopped down in the chair Riley vacated not an hour before. Her jeans had holes in the knees where they'd thinned over time and her shirt was one of Fame's castoffs, a flannel plaid what'd shrunk from being run through the wash once too many. A golden ring hung from a chain around her neck. Its solid inset ruby glinted outta the gap in her shirt in the trailer's uneven light.

"Will you ever tire of that joke?" she asked.

"Not any time soon," I said, cheerful like. "What's for supper?"

"Roast ham, baby potatoes from the garden, and fresh green beans," she said, so automatic I raised an eyebrow. "I enjoy feeding my family. That doesn't mean Fame chains me to the stove."

"Missy, honey, you're barefoot and spend most of your time in the kitchen. If you was pregnant, you'd be the perfect Southern woman."

A cloud crossed her expression, quick and black, and was smoothed over by a gentle smile. "Someday, maybe."

I snorted. "You want kids, you're gonna have to kick Fame in the rear to get 'em. You ain't getting no younger. Don't pussy foot around or you'll never have them babies."

Her smile turned arch and mischief filled them violet eyes. "Oh? And what about you, Sunshine? Are you making plans to have babies with that handsome young man who left here a while ago?"

I choked out a laugh even as my nethers tightened and burned. Riley's kids, held gentle and safe in my womb, and the deeds we'd have to do to plant 'em there? I'd never have that, not on the coldest day in hell or the warmest in Heaven. Didn't matter none. Henry had been enough, even for the short time he'd been mine, God rest him.

"Not likely," I said.

"So he was here on business, then."

The good humor Missy spread like wildfire snapped right outta me. "Seems something's disturbing the high and mighty out on Burton. I told him no."

"And he accepted that?" She shook her head, jiggling the sable curls piled willy-nilly onto her crown. "Seemed like the persistent sort to me."

I flopped into my own chair, slumping with my arms and legs akimbo. "He asked me to dinner. Steaks at his house. Think he mighta wanted more."

She leaned forward, expression glowing with rapt interest. "Do tell."

I shrugged. "Ain't nothing to say. Men only want two things outta me and neither one is fit to speak on in polite company."

"Oh, honey, don't be that way. You're a good woman, Sunshine. You are," she added when I sneered. "Don't put yourself down like that."

"All I'm doing is holding on to reality. Ever body knows I'm a stone cold killer, just like my mama."

"That's not..." Missy sighed and pressed her lips together, firm as they ever got. "I bet he wanted more than a quick roll in the hay."

"Oh, I bet it woulda been kinda long and drawn out like, rumor holds true," I said, and she laughed like I intended her to. Missy was the kind of woman nobody ever wanted to see go without a smile for long. "Anyhow, it ain't no never mind to me. Riley Treadwell ain't somebody what orta be spending time around here nohow."

"Sheriff Treadwell's son, the one that got back from the Army, what, four years ago or so now?"

"The very same. He might come back." I give a half-hearted laugh at her pointed look. "Wants me to do that job something fierce, so I reckon he'll show up on my stoop in a few days. Warn Fame, wouldja? Don't want the boys getting in no trouble."

"Those boys are your age, Sunshine. When are you going to start calling them men?"

"When they grow up," I said, and grinned.

Her smile went wry. Missy had at least two dozen different kinds of smile, and she wore ever one of 'em when she talked. "I'm going into town later for a grocery run. You need anything?"

"The usual." I shored up my courage and blurted out, "You want company?"

She rose in that slow way she had, all ladylike and graceful, like she was wearing a fancy gown and a tiara instead of threadbare hand-me-downs. "Only if you want to tag along, and I know you don't."

I stood up, offered my cheek for a kiss, and sensed what always come to me around her. Fresh mowed grass in the spring, the musty damp of a closed in tomb, the faint clash of swords on a battlefield. No idea what it meant. Didn't care, neither. Missy's past weren't none of my beeswax.

'Sides, I kinda liked having her close. She was my friend, near about the only one I had. If I let on like I was catching them glimpses, she was sure to hightail it outta here, and then where'd we be? No Missy with her warm smiles and generous curves, no woman friend to lean on and be leaned on in return.

Plus, her and Fame and the boys, they was my family and about the limit of my tolerance for touching. I relented ever once in a while and went into the city after a man. Good Book or no, a woman had needs, though mine went untended often as not. Still, a body needed human contact, down in the soul where we forgot to tend. Reckon that's why Riley Treadwell turned me on the way he did.

'Course, that didn't explain why he always had.

"Be careful," I said. "Likely get rain later and traffic's bound to be awful, what with the holiday and all."

"Only in town." She glided to the door, peeked at me coy like over her shoulder, her violet eyes lit by a strange light. "Riley Treadwell comes around again, you think hard before turning him down."

"Go on with you now, Missy," I said, gentle enough to dull the sting of my words. Ten to one, nobody'd ever treated her like she was no better'n the muck on the bottom of their shoes, even now with her and Fame living in sin. Missy's goodness shone outta her like a beacon, warming ever body stepping crossways over the path her elegant feet trod. She weren't no backwoods trash, the mixed breed daughter of a man what'd run off to be with another man and the woman what'd carved 'em both into puzzle pieces with a dull butcher knife.

I watched Missy leave and envied her something fierce in that place where Henry lived, and then I let it fly free like a good Christian would. Too bad me and the Christ child was on the outs or that small gesture mighta earned me some points, evening out the pile of sins stacked high all around me.

2

I made a PB and honey, strapped on my Ruger 1911, and carried my supper out to the spot on the trail where Henry disappeared more'n three years ago. Over time, we cut out a place alongside the trail, erected a small marker with his name on it. Added a bench so we could visit him, catch him up on the goings on. Missy planted flowers, gobs of 'em all around, turning the tiny memorial into a park. About a year ago, I found a concrete angel no bigger'n my knee to the ground and hauled it out. Now, it watched over Henry when I couldn't.

I sat on the bench and seeped myself in the silence for a minute, alone with the birds chirping and the squirrels stirring the underbrush. It was peaceful out here, restful now that summer was dying and fall was tiptoeing in. Sometimes, if I closed my eyes real tight and wished with all my mama's heart, I could about feel my boy hovering nearby, his face lit up with a smile and them big ol' ears twitching when he laughed. Lord, them ears was about big enough to fly away on, like Dumbo only on a little boy.

Henry'd loved Dumbo.

I closed my eyes and reached out a hand, searching for that feeling, sending out my love to him. *I miss you so much, Henry,* I thought, and drew my hand in to swipe away the water leaking outta my eyes. Henry was the first person what ever loved me, was mine alone anyhow. He never cared none about me being a no account piece of trash, never spent a minute thinking on how I was anything outside of his mama.

That woulda changed when he went off to school, once he was around gossip and spite. I managed to hold him close to home 'til he was past Kindergarten, sheltering him from the hurt I knowed was coming. Taught him his three R's myself, sitting out on the front porch playing cards and Yahtzee or reading a book. Lordy, we had a load of fun, did me and Henry.

After that, though, I was scared DFACS would come 'round and claim I was unfit or some such, so I done my duty and registered him for first grade, brung Henry in and introduced him real adult like to his teacher down at the new school. Miss Jenny Brookshire. She weren't from around here, claimed no kin nearby, as I recalled. Henry took a real shine to her and she to him, seemed like. He was all excited about riding that big ol' yellow bus and making new friends and learning.

Henry was always one to stick his mind to something when it caught his interest.

I scraped together enough money to take him shopping down at the Mall of Georgia, first time I ever been, and the last, too. Got him some real nice clothes, washed 'em up and tucked 'em away in that old dresser of Daddy's, and then I made the mistake what got Henry killed. I trusted the deep wood.

I'm sorry, baby. So, so sorry.

A quiet thud hit the trail twenty feet away, 'round the

bend toward Fame's, and the critters hushed. I opened my eyes, eased my hand toward the 1911 strapped over my hip. Since that pooka, we never went nowhere in the deep wood without a weapon. You hear a rustle out here, could be a painter or a bear, or could be something a whole heckuva lot worse.

Fame strode 'round the bend, his dishwater blond hair sticking up ever which way, like he just tumbled outta bed. He weren't careful, Missy'd be after him with her scissors. No telling what he'd look like when she got done neither. She was a good cook and could make any plant grow fast as a weed, but we learnt real quick like not to bow our heads under her scissors. Missy had a habit of letting her mind wander and her hands with it.

Fame dropped down on the bench beside me and slung an arm along the top behind my back. His wild blue eyes landed on Henry's stone and stuck there. "Hey, Sunny girl. Figured I'd find you here."

"I was eating lunch with Henry, 'bout to share some gossip."

"Yeah? Anything good?"

"Belinda Arrowood, you remember her? She was a Heaton from Satolah what married Tom Arrowood and took on his two girls to raise."

Fame grunted. Tom'd helped us out of a tricky spot or two with the law over the years. More particular, he'd helped Fame's boys outta some minor drug possession charges. They was pretty careful to steer clear of the law, but nobody could avoid 'em one hundred percent of the time, 'specially when the sheriff was gunning for you.

"Anyhow," I said, "I reckon she got some property over on Burton. Heard tale something's tearing up her dock."

"That why Riley Treadwell was sniffing around your trailer today?"

"He weren't sniffing, Fame, he was asking. Said Belinda was a paying client." I crossed my arms over my bitty breasts.

They'd perked up a bit on hearing Riley's name and I weren't wearing no bra to hide the evidence. "I could use the money."

"You need money, you come to me." Fame's voice mighta been soft, but underneath lay pure steel. Weren't no love lost between the Carsons and the Treadwells, and sure as tootin', weren't none lost between me and that hussy Belinda. "Ain't no call to mess with the likes of her."

"Come on, Fame. You knowed I was gonna have to work with the uppity folk when this begun. Ain't no other way to do it around here."

"You ain't gotta do that kind of work, hon."

My eyes caught on the angel guarding over my boy. "You know that ain't so, Fame. You know it ain't."

He sighed and tucked me in to him, wrapped his strong arm around my shoulder and hugged hard. "I know, Sunny. God'd listen, I'd wish it all away. Henry was a good young'un."

I sniffed and nodded, stiffened my trembling lips.

"You coming up for supper?" he asked.

"Probably." Mischief poked at me, easing through the weight of guilt and sorrow. "You cooking?"

"Hell, Sunny, why tempt the devil to happy, sending one of us down?" He ruffled my hair with one of his narrow hands, like he done when I was a kid. "I got something to show you, you come up."

"Must be something bad if it brung you to me."

"Might be. Something strange in the water. Could be my imagination, though."

That weren't likely. Fame was serious about his water. Bad water made bad liquor, and he had a reputation for the good. "I can run up tonight before dark, you want."

"'Preciate it." He give me another good squeeze. "I gotta go round up them boys, move a little merchandise around before that feller of yourn comes sniffing around again."

Merchandise, my hiney. He was moving plants. "Tell the

boys not to put any on my land. One of us has got to stay clean to get the other outta jail."

"You just don't want that Treadwell boy busting you with it." He stood and looked down on me with them wild eyes of his, crazy as a mad boar and twice as mean, 'less you was family. His mouth turned up into what mighta been a smile. "Missy said you got the hots for him."

"Jesus, Fame," I said, and winced. Dagnabbit. Another quarter for my jar, twice in one day, and all 'cause of Riley Treadwell. "I ain't got the hots for him. He brung me a potential client, is all."

"Way I hear tell, that ain't all he brung you."

I was gonna kill Missy deader'n a doorknob, family or no. "You want me to check your dang water or not?"

"You always was easy to rile." He laid a hand on my crown, smoothed it over my stick straight hair. "Come up for supper. We ain't seen enough outta you here of late."

"I'll be there."

I watched him walk away, his booted feet near silent on the spongy bed of the trail. Thing about Fame was, he loved his family and was loyal to the bone. He passed that on to us young'uns, taught us what he could of right and wrong. Him taking me in after Mama chopped Daddy into sushi, that was right. Me going after what killed my baby, that was right, too. Didn't matter none if the Carsons and the Treadwells rubbed the wrong kinda sparks off each other. If there was something out there liable to hurt an innocent, I had to go after it. Fame understood, even if he didn't much like the company I kept while I was a-going.

'Course, I hadn't decided whether I was gonna help Riley or not, and through him, Belinda. Snooping didn't count. Weren't nothing to that and I enjoyed it anyhow. Didn't mean I was gonna lend a helping hand to the woman what'd made my teen years hell. Truth be told, I'd as soon not, paying client or no.

I sighed, pulled my sandwich outta its hankie, and

chewed on it whilst my brain chewed on ever thing else.

THE AFTERNOON whizzed by. I puttered in the house, straightened my work files, dusted off Daddy's LP collection. Didn't hardly play 'em none. They was too precious to me, one of the few things left of him 'sides memory. I did turn on the local radio station, hoping to catch the news. Instead, I caught an earful of cringe-worthy pop.

Lord all mighty, what was them musicians thinking, making that racket? I mean, I knowed the Good Book said to make a joyful noise and all, but I couldn't find a dadgum thing joyful in the beeboppy dance tunes sputtering outta the radio's speakers.

As if the DJ heard my complaints, a Journey song come on just as I was filing the last album back in its place. I sprawled into my desk chair and listened it out, eyes closed. Missy was likely waiting supper on me, but that weren't no excuse to waste a good Journey song when one come along.

Once the song was done, I cleaned up best I could, stuck a mini-Maglite in my back pocket behind the 1911, and trudged up to Fame's along the trail worn by the feet of me and my kin. The deep wood cast a long shadow over the ground as the sun worked its way close to the mountaintops. At Henry's marker, I touched my fingertips to my lips, then to the top of the stone as I wandered past.

'Bout the time I rounded the bend and spotted the shabby single-wide Fame called home, the scent of baked ham tickled my nose. I lengthened my steps up the slight slope toward the trailer, eager for a taste of Missy's good home cooking. Weren't like I weren't always welcome. I was, but a body could only handle so much family time with this bunch. Trey drove me half mad with his mischief and Gentry, well. He was a sweet'un, but he weren't exactly the brightest bulb. Was a time I wished for a normal family like Riley's, one what spent their time at barbecues and card playing, not growing dope and running from the law.

'Course, that was before I learnt what kinda man Sheriff Treadwell was. Not a bad'un, just not much of a good'un either. It was also a long time before I learnt that sometimes what's on the outside ain't near as important as what's tucked into heart and bone.

The front door popped open and Gentry stuck his head out, his normally affable expression twisted into a frown. "Hurry up, Sunny. Missy's in a tizzy."

I jogged up the steps onto the wooden porch set like an afterthought in front of the door and pushed my way past Gentry's solid girth. Missy sat at the tiny table in the dining area with Fame stooped over her running a soothing hand along her back. Her hands trembled and tears leaked outta her violet eyes onto her cheeks, and it was about all I could do to stand there and watch.

What in tarnation was so bad it made Missy cry?

She caught sight of me and held out a graceful hand. "Oh, Sunny. You won't believe what happened. My ring's gone."

I glanced at the spot on her chest where it normally rested. The space was empty, chain and all. I crossed the room, took her hand, and knelt down in front of her. "When did it go a-missing?"

Her hand squeezed around mine, so tight I bit back a gasp. She touched her other hand to her chest where the ring shoulda been. "In Ingles, I think. I was standing in line waiting for the Rhone boy to finish ringing up the customer in front of me. Such a polite young man. You know him, Sunny. His daddy manages the quarry and his mama is president of the Garden Club."

"Missy," I said, gentle as I could. Lordy, if I didn't interrupt her, she'd go on all day about who was who and what was what. "What happened to the ring?"

"I don't know." Her voice dropped to a hoarse whisper. "I felt a little tug at my neck. I thought maybe the chain had come undone and the ring had dropped into my shirt, but there was nothing there. It was just gone."

"Was anybody around you?"

She shook her head, sending sable curls tumbling around her ears. "Not a soul, as far as I could tell. Oh, Sunny. What am I going to do? That ring was an heirloom, an antique. It was *special* and now I've lost it."

I stood abruptly and glanced toward Trey and Gentry. For once, they stood quiet like outta the way, their expressions twin seats of misery. I knowed exactly how they felt. Nobody liked to see Missy cry.

"What you done to find it?" I asked.

Trey scrubbed a broad palm over his unruly, dishwater blond hair. "Searched the car and the parking area. Gentry hiked up and down the trails where Missy normally walks. Dad called Ingles."

"Said they'd keep a sharp eye out," Fame said, his voice quiet and calm. "Only a fool'd turn that ring in, though."

That was for sure. Missy's ring was solid gold. I was pretty sure the ruby was real, too, and it was big enough to tempt the sweetest saint.

I patted Missy's hand, attempting comfort. "I was gonna run into town tomorrow. Reckon I could canvass the pawn shops, get word out about the ring."

Fame's lips curled into a smile, half sneer, half amusement. "Nobody fucks the Carsons over."

"If somebody took it, chances is good they don't know who she is. Don't you worry none, Missy. It'll turn up, soon as word gets 'round." I crossed my arms over my chest and looked over the half-prepared meal with a resigned sigh. "All righty, then. Looks like me and the boys'll be finishing up supper tonight."

I dropped a kiss to Missy's forehead, slipped off my jacket, and rolled up my sleeves. It weren't that I hated cooking. That weren't it a'tall. It's just that cooking for one is about as appealing as walking knee deep in rotten fish guts, so

I didn't spend much time in the kitchen, though I knowed my way around it well enough. Mama mighta been stone cold crazy, but she done right by me where the womanly arts was concerned. I could whip up a decent meal, sew a straight seam by hand and machine, and nobody but nobody ever had a bad word to say about the state of my house.

Being dirt poor weren't no excuse for keeping an untidy roost. That's what Mama said anyhow.

My reason for being there didn't hit me 'til after we squeezed in around the tiny kitchen table and tucked into supper. "You got them water samples for me, Fame?"

"In the shed." He ducked his head towards Missy and said, "Eat, baby."

"I'm trying, Fame." She touched her head to his and closed her eyes. "What would I do without you?"

He murmured something too low to hear what brought a wavering smile to her face. I dropped my own eyes to my plate and hid a smile behind a fork full of taters. That's what I loved about Fame and Missy. They was good together. I ignored the small shaft of envy worming its way up my innards. Some folks was blessed with the love they found. Someday, I might be, too.

Soon as the meal was finished, I left cleanup to the boys and followed Fame out back to the storage shed he converted into a workspace slash laboratory when we was kids. Not many folks knowed it, but Fame was right smart when he put his mind to something. He went to Georgia Tech on a full scholarship and studied chemistry before his daddy up and died, leaving Fame's mama, my granny, with a house full of young'uns to raise and no way to pay the bills. Fame'd put his chemistry degree to good use by going into the family business making illicit 'shine. Unlike Grampy Carson, he run a clean still using only the best ingredients, including the water.

Soon as we went inside the shed, Fame pulled out a sheaf of papers and handed 'em to me. I handed 'em right back. "Give it to me in plain English, Fame, not geek speak."

"Pollution what ain't supposed to be there."

It was simple enough, but the only question I could land on was, what kind of pollution was *supposed* to be in the water? I turned it over in my noggin a bit and finally settled on something a sight more innocuous. "Where'd you find this again?"

"Half a mile up the creek. Sheen on the water is what got me to testing it." He gathered the tests and water vials together, handed those to me like I knowed what I was looking at. "I searched another half mile upstream and didn't find nothing. I was hoping you'd take some time to look into it, maybe see if you can find the source."

I stared at the vials holding the tainted water and the papers holding the results of his tests, and my mind wiggled and hummed. "Reckon I could walk up a ways more, see what's what. Not tomorrow, though. Got business in town."

"That business include Riley Treadwell?"

"You ever gonna let that bone go?"

"Not as long as it puts pink in your cheeks."

"Hunh. Serve you right if I took him up on his offer."

Fame's gaze sharpened on mine. "What offer?"

"Steaks on the grill and baked sweet potatoes." I left out the part where I thought Riley mighta wanted something else. No need to give Fame another reason to hate the Treadwells when the Sheriff seeded that ground all by his lonesome. "Could be I orta butter him up anyhow, what with the water going sour."

"We can take care of our own, Sunny girl," he said, and that was the end of that.

Still, I mulled it over during the walk back home. Like it or not, Riley was in the perfect position to help me figure out what was in the water. Me, I'd have to cajole and threaten to get answers. Riley had the power of the law behind him and was charming to boot, when he put his mind to it.

I flicked the flashlight over the ground and pushed down the anticipation building low in my gut. Sure as tootin', he'd be 'round soon to spread a little more charm my way for one reason or another. Sooner I prepared myself for it, the better off I'd be.

3

The next day, I dressed in a black, short sleeved t-shirt, jeans, and boots, fired up Daddy's IROC, and headed into town. Clayton weren't much of nothing to look on. Folks sure did whiz through it fast enough on the highway. The real draw was the mountains surrounding the town, softened under time's unceasing touch, and the hiking trails, camping areas, and waterways running ever which way through the sloping hills. The upcoming Labor Day holiday just three days away represented summer's last big hoorah for most of the city bred tourists clamoring for space in the crowded woods. After that'd come the leaf lookers, folks what thought the changing leaves put on too spectacular a show to miss.

Sometimes I wanted to roll down my window as I was driving by picture takers and shout, *Ain't you got no leaves back home?* But Missy told me that weren't politic, so I clamped my mouth shut and let them poor suckers be.

I stopped in at the public library first since it was on my way. I requested recent back issues of the *Tribune* at the circulation desk and slumped into a chair at a nearby table to thumb through 'em. Clayton's so small, the paper weren't hardly ever more'n three sections deep, sometimes not even that, and it usually weren't more'n twenty pages total. It only come out once a week, which orta tell anybody how much goes on in the county. It didn't take long to skim through the good news (the oldest daughter of Cousin Ricky Dean on Mama's side won an essay contest at school) and the bad (Cousin Ricky Dean got picked up by a Sheriff's Deputy for dealing meth) for a whole month's worth of news.

I shook my head at Ricky Dean's antics and kept digging, and finally found an interesting tidbit in July's final paper. Buried on page A-10 was a two-paragraph update about a twenty-year old woman what'd gone missing in mid-June while night swimming off her family's dock at Lake Burton. Some summer folks found her wandering the woods two days before the paper went to press, babbling nonsense about offerings and wearing a brand-spanking-new swirling tattoo on her neck. I scrounged up some scrap paper and a pencil from the circulation desk and jotted down all the details, then requested June's papers and tracked down the original article reporting her going missing.

It was on the front page. Apparently, being found didn't rate near as high in the news world as getting lost.

I went back clear through March and didn't find another drop of news about the lake outside charity functions and society news. Once I turned all the papers back in, I dug through the map cabinet and located an old Forest Service map showing the water courses around Fame's land, just to refresh my memory on which ones was connected to what and how best to access 'em.

While I was at it, I dug another topo out and pinpointed Greenwood Cove's location along the lake. If I was gonna snoop into Belinda's business, I might as well snoop right.

The cove was located in a secluded section of the lake a quarter of the way down its length from the dam, off Charlie Mountain Road on what looked like a tiny, unmarked lane. Leastwise, no name was attached to it on the map. I sketched the road's lay on a scrap piece of paper fetched from the desk, then studied the map 'til it was stuck in my memory.

When I was done, I spent a precious few minutes browsing the new releases. John Ringo had a new book out. I picked it up, thumbed through it, and scowled. Dagnabbit. I missed the last one. Now I'd have to request it before I could read the newest. I propped the book back on its shelf and headed into the stacks toward fiction, hoping against hope that the library had the book on site.

Halfway back, I near about run over Jenny Brookshire. My breath whooshed out in a rush. Last time I seen her was about two days before the deep wood took Henry.

She stopped in front of me, her gray eyes wide, her hands clenched tight around a stack of half a dozen books. Likely, she was remembering the last time she saw me, too, and regretting running into me.

Death has that effect on most folks, 'specially a tragic death like Henry's. *So young,* people said. *So full of promise.* Least that's what the kinder folk murmured when they seen me. I didn't like to dwell on what ever body else had to say.

"Sunny." Jenny bobbled her books and righted them with a breathy laugh. "It's so good to see you. How have you been?"

"I been right good, Miss Jenny. How's school a-going?"

"Oh, well, you know. It's going." She laughed again, this'un more genuine. "The kids are still excited. In another month, they'll have settled into a routine and school won't be nearly as fun."

I remembered that feeling, the newness of fall's start wearing off under the daily grind of sitting still and doing homework. A small silence drifted over us and I scrambled for another topic. My eyes fell on her books. "Homer?"

"I was in the mood for a little Greek history. One of my minors was in the Classics and I have so much time on my hands since my fiancé left." She cleared her throat and glanced away, and her cheeks took on the pink Fame accused me of wearing when I thought on Riley. "Well, I have a lot of time right now."

"I'm sorry, Miss Jenny."

Her eyes jerked back to mine and went round as saucers. "Oh, no. Don't be. It was for the best all the way around. I didn't mean to mention it."

I grinned. "Lotta stuff pops outta my mouth I don't mean to mention, neither."

"That makes two of us then." She smiled and shifted the books in her hands. "I should get these checked out before my arm muscles give out. It was nice seeing you again, Sunny."

"You, too, Miss Jenny. You take care now."

"I shall."

I turned and followed her progress to the circulation desk, made sure she didn't trip over her own two feet and sprawl head first into the thin carpet. She sure was a nice woman. Too bad about her fiancé. In my experience, most men didn't know a good thing when they had it, and I reckoned that was the case with Miss Jenny. Then again, maybe it was as she said and for the best.

I spared a few more minutes picking out a book (military SciFi; the John Ringo book put me in the mood), checked it out at the circulation desk, then headed out to Injun Bob's Pawn Shoppe and Fine Antiques, better known as Clayton's biggest junk store.

Injun Bob weren't really no injun and he sure as tootin' weren't named Bob. The name he usually answered to was Oakleaf Bunnyhopper, but I was pretty near certain that weren't his legal name neither. Injun Bob was a product of the '60s, and that explained a lot about him. Anyhow, he was long gone, travelling the world in a beat up Vanagon while his granddaughter BobbiJean tended the store. I went to school with her boyfriend Jazz, him what run a scrap metal business out back of Injun Bob's where he created some mighty fine folk art in between recycling worn out washers and dryers.

A bell rattled merrily as I stepped into the store. The place was crowded from one end to the other with an odd assortment of junk. Musical instruments of all shapes, sizes, and conditions occupied the entire wall to the right, tools and small appliances the entire wall on the left. In between was stereo systems, boxes of LPs, CDs, cassettes, and eight-tracks, fur coats I figured was genuine, and a playpen full of stuffed animals. Kewpie dolls stood shoulder to shoulder with action figures, a complete set of heavy duty tires was laid down in the middle aisle like an obstacle course, and old quilts was draped willy-nilly in and around everything. I picked my way through the tires, rifled through a box of comic books tucked behind a hula girl lamp, and rubbed a sneeze outta my nose what was stirred up by the fine layer of dust coating the shelves.

BobbiJean popped outta the door set into the back wall behind the glass counter running the width of the far end of the store. "Hey, Sunny. Long time no see!"

"I was just in here last month."

"Yeah, but I didn't get to see you."

She dusted her hands off on her jeans and settled onto a wooden stool behind the cash register. I sidled closer, took a good gander at her jeans, and snickered. "Jazz moved on to roosters, huh."

She rolled her eyes. "Honest to goodness, I don't have a single pair of pants left that he hasn't painted. I guess I was lucky he stuck with something tame like barnyard animals."

That was true enough. Jazz had gone through a nigh on unforgettable phase in high school where he painted penises on everything. Animal penises, human penises, big, small, straight, and crooked. If it was a penis, he painted it, and he didn't spare a thought for the surface he used, neither. He got suspended for painting erections on the back of the vice principal's new sedan, complete with testicles and anatomically correct veins, but that was after I dropped outta school to have Henry. Too bad, too. It woulda been a sight to see.

"You here for a reason or did you just come to chat?" BobbiJean asked.

"A little of both." I dug the drawing I sketched of Missy's ring outta the front pocket of my very plain jeans and handed it to her. "Fame's girlfriend Missy lost this ring yesterday, maybe in Ingles. We was hoping it'd turn up in the pawn shops."

"I'll keep an eye out for it."

"Call Fame if somebody brings it in, wouldja?"

"Will do. Speaking of rings." She tucked the drawing away under a corner of the cash register and leaned her elbows on the counter. Her doe brown eyes took on a happy twinkle as she wiggled the fingers of her left hand at me. "Jazz asked me to marry him."

"Well, there's something I never thought to hear." I touched a finger to the simple metal band twining 'round her ring finger and ignored the envy sinking into my gut. "He made it?"

"Hammered it out of a nickel. It was the sweetest thing." She heaved a contented sigh and grabbed my hand, holding it tight in hers. "We're doing the deed next month. You'll come, won't you?"

"Oh, I don't know, BobbiJean. Me and crowds don't get on too well together."

Her round face set into determined lines. "Sunshine Walkingstick, you better not be trying to wiggle out of coming to my wedding."

I hunched my shoulders and shot her a sheepish grin. "Nothing like that, I sworn."

"Wear a dress and bring a date," she said firmly. "A real man, too, with a newish car and a job and all his own teeth."

"Hey, now. Harley Jimpson was a client, not a date, and

I wouldn'ta touched him with a ten-foot pole if Fame hadn'ta owed him a favor."

She grinned and settled back on the stool. "Jazz wants you there, too. Oh, say you'll come, Sunny. We're having a country band and hayrides and a bonfire, and we're hoping to get a quart or two of Fame's best corn liquor to liven things up a bit."

"You send me the invite and I'll show up with bells on," I promised, though I didn't swear to the date and the dress. Some things was beyond my control. "The liquor's on me."

We chatted a few minutes more, about the wedding and Jazz's plans to refurbish the tuxedo he wore to his senior prom with a few coats of paint. That alone was worth going to the wedding for. I asked if BobbiJean heard any news of strange goings-on down at the lake and she said no, though she promised to holler at me if she did. I left feeling a mite better'n I had in a while. Trust them two to put a smile on a woman's face.

I MADE THE ROUNDS through the other pawn shops in Clayton proper, spreading the word about Missy's ring, and dropped into Ingles with a reminder to call if the ring turned up. By the time I was finished, hunger had gnawed a fist sized hole in my belly. I pulled into the drive through at Micky D's and ordered two cheeseburgers off the dollar menu and a small coke, then headed back toward home, eating as I drove. There was plenty of daylight left when I hit Timpson Creek, so I signaled and turned left onto Charlie Mountain Road.

I didn't know much about Tom Arrowood other'n what spread on the grapevine and what he done for Fame's boys. Rumor had it he drunk his fill of liquor and showed up for court sloshed to the gills often as not, that he cheated on his first wife before she died of breast cancer eight years back, and that Belinda used her real estate earnings to bail him outta serious financial trouble when they got hitched four years later. He had two daughters by his first wife. I reckoned Belinda was too frigid to spread her legs often enough to get a babe in her belly, or maybe she was too worried about retaining her girlish figure.

Either way, the lake property was his, passed down from his grandparents or some such. Belinda had blabbed her mouth when they tied the knot about how she brung in fancy folk from Atlanta to do the place up. Made it into a showcase, I heard. Likely, she'd get it in the divorce, which was sure to come in another year or two. Tom was husband number three for Belinda, and she weren't but a year older'n me. I didn't see her sticking by a lush after she bled him dry like she done her first two misters.

I almost missed the turn into the cove, so bitter was my thoughts, and that's what I got for dwelling on the past instead of facing the future. I whipped the IROC in and followed the road 'til I spotted the sign for the Arrowood house. The parking lot was empty when I pulled in, and I didn't feel bad a'tall for making myself to home there.

I never seen the original house, but the one in front of me seemed a mite small for a woman as snooty and pretentious as Belinda. It was two stories or so. Its board and batten siding was painted a sedate forest green with tan paint on the trim. A porch fenced in by wooden railing jutted off the front and hung over the steep slope from the house to the water. I wound my way through the evenly spaced shrubbery and jumped over the locked gate.

They wanted folks out, maybe they orta built the dang railing more'n waist high.

Wooden steps twisted and turned down to the water, pausing in three places where small decks was situated at irregular intervals. Belinda, or likely the guy what kept their lawn, had placed big ol' pots of plants on the edges of the decks around wooden benches and tables. The effect was surprisingly inviting. Next time, I'd carry my camera along and take pictures for Missy. She was all the time oohing over stuff like this in them home and garden magazines she borrowed from the library.

The series of stairs and decks ended on a large rectangular one attached to a boathouse. I laid down flat, held my hair back with one hand, and peered under the deck at the pilings. The water was up too high for me to see much. The power company controlling the lake usually left it full in the summer to please visitors, including them with second homes.

The blue-brown water lapped at the top of the pilings less than a foot below my dangling head, reflecting the sun back in sharp glints. I slithered around on my belly for a better angle and lucked out on my third try. About two or three feet below the water's surface, a large splinter of wood stuck out from one of the pilings. I squinted at it and finally decided the piling itself was dented, though I couldn't be sure unless I jumped into the water. Now, I was a strong enough swimmer, but I weren't willing to strip down to my skivvies and dive in without a swim buddy. That and I didn't wanna smell like lake water 'til I got home.

I pushed myself into a stand and clomped out onto the floating dock attached to the deck. About a man's length from the end, I halted in mid-stride and stared at the crumpled wood making up the last few feet. The boards was cracked smack dab down the middle and turned into a vee, like something heavy'd landed on 'em. I sidestepped to the edge, peered into the water, and sighed. Couldn't see a dadgum thing through the murk.

A boat roared across the cove's opening. I glanced up, watched it pass, then studied the four other docks poking into the water around Belinda and Tom's. Two of 'em was messed up same as theirs. From where I stood, I could easily make out a dent in a neighboring boathouse, kinda like something big rammed it just below the water's surface.

A bare foot slapped onto the dock behind me. I whirled around, heart in my throat, and goggled at the man staring back at me. He musta been six foot tall, maybe thirty-five or forty, and was long and lean, muscled yeah, but not heavy with it. His black hair was slicked back and a black goatee decorated his square chin. He weren't wearing nothing outside of baggy white swim trunks what was soaking wet and clung to his legs.

My mouth went dry. Lordy, it'd been a coon's age since I seen a man's nekkid chest muscles, and his was something to behold. They looked like they was sculpted by hand and had not one curl of hair marring the sleek, wet lines.

I yanked my eyes up to his amused ones. "Howdy there."

"Hello." His voice was low and smooth, and held a trace of a foreign accent I couldn't quite put my finger on. "You're trespassing."

I grinned, unoffended. He was right, for one, and for another, I weren't the only trespasser standing on that dock. "Sunny Walkingstick. A friend of Belinda asked me if I'd come check out the damage to her dock."

He nodded solemnly, though his wide mouth held a hint of a smile. "Abercio Okeanos. I am a...business acquaintance of the Arrowood family."

I let the slight hesitation pass. I hadn't decided yet whether I wanted to help Miss High and Mighty out or not, and 'til then, I weren't speculating on Mr. Okeanos' presence. "Ya don't say. Well. I seen what I needed to. Reckon I'll be on my way."

I walked by him real casual like, though my heart still jittered and hopped. Handsome is as handsome does, I reminded myself, and promptly squashed the thought that I had to find a date for Jazz and BobbiJean's wedding. This'un was probably Belinda's lover. At the very least, he'd be on her short list of future husbands.

His hand flashed out and caught my arm in a firm grip. "Sunshine."

I glanced at him outta the corner of my eye. "That's me."

"I adore the sun shining on the water, the way it reflects off the waves and lights the sodden depths." His thumb rubbed slow circles over the bare skin of my upper arm, and my skin tingled and warmed. "Join me?"

"Ah, maybe another time, Mr. Okeanos. Water's a little cold for me this time of year."

He leaned closer and a whiff of saltwater floated over me, not the stench of the freshwater lake, but the hint of mist floating over the sea. "I can keep you warm, Sunny."

I shivered. Holy moly. Did he come on to every woman he met that heavy? If he did, there must be a string of 'em begging for more trailed out years deep. "I really gotta get home now, sir."

"Sir," he repeated, humor heavy in the single word. He slid his hand down my arm, caught my fingers in his, then lifted them to his mouth for a lingering kiss. "You, my beauty, must call me Teus."

Tay-oos. I shivered again and reclaimed my hand, polite as I could, which is to say, I jerked it away from him like he singed me. I turned and walked up the dock toward the house as fast as I could without seeming to rush, took the steps two at a time as my heart was still a-pounding something fierce in my chest. I hadn't made it to the second oddly placed deck when his voice halted me.

"Sunshine," he called. "I'll see you next Friday."

I gripped the wooden railing and stared down at him. "What's happening next Friday?"

"We shall dance."

He eased to the edge of the dock, leapt backward in a high, graceful arch, and slipped into the water hands first without a single splash.

I blinked at the water where he'd disappeared. Holy moly. I shoulda went with him, just to see him do that again.

I shook the thought off along with the odd feelings lingering after Teus' touch and jogged up the last section of steps. Him, I had to tell Missy about. Goodness knowed she needed a pick me up. The mighty handsome Teus fit the bill to a tee.

4

I didn't get a chance to talk to Missy that night. Was too late to go up the hill by the time I hit home, so I fixed some supper and let the problem of her ring rest for a bit.

First thing the next day, I lit out exploring the waterways upstream of the creek Fame siphoned his liquor water off of, Daddy's hunting knife strapped to my ankle like it always was. I added the 1911 to my hip, not knowing where the day'd carry me. I tucked a clean change of clothes, a towel, and an extra pair of shoes into the IROC before heading out. The trek through the woods was liable to get muddy, if I didn't fall elbow over arse into the water first.

Fame said when I was in Heaven waiting to be born, I musta passed through the line for clumsiness twice.

The morning was mild with the promise of a hot, humid afternoon ahead. September in the mountains didn't mean cold like it did up north. It just meant we might draw a cleaner breath under the heavy afternoon sun than we did at the height of summer.

It was a short drive to the best access point for investigating our creek. Driving cut out a lot of the plain ol' walking time I woulda done if I'da just gone from home, and it weren't like anybody'd steal my ride. I made my way to the headwaters of the creek first, backtracking over what Fame'd already checked, and found not a cussed thing, no dumping or signs of campers, not nothing. Weren't so much as a leaf outta place, far as I could tell, and I been up and down the creek enough to know.

When I hit the headwaters, I one-eightyed and headed back the way I come. I walked to where the creek dumped into Howard Branch, then turned and walked to its headwaters and back. I found a dead frog and the bones of a small critter what'd died in the water. Couldn't tell what kinda critter without getting soaked. Not much else, though, and I figured a dead pond hopper weren't reason enough to raise no alarm.

I wended my way through the woods to my car and drove out Patterson Gap Road. Weren't hard to pick out little spots 'long and along for parking. The walk through the woods was another matter all together. Some spots, the undergrowth was so thick I could scarce push through it, and more'n once, the surrounding slopes prevented me from walking the waterway itself. I zigzagged up the creek in short jigs. Park the IROC, push my way to the creek, trudge around searching for anything what might give me a clue as to why Fame found that odd sheen, fight the laurel and weeds back to the car, and start all over again.

I seen that same sheen a time or two, mostly in the still parts where the current slowed and the water deepened. Seen a handful of dead fish, too, little runts no bigger'n my hand, about all the creek'd support through here. Didn't have an extra bag in the car or I woulda picked 'em up and took 'em back to Fame for testing. Maybe whatever was tainting the water was killing the fish. Coulda been another reason they was floating belly up. Didn't seem none too likely, though.

I done that trek for half the morning before I finally hit the spot where Howard Branch dumped into Persimmon Creek. There weren't a lick of anything suspicious along that section. I stuck my hands on my hips and studied the confluence real careful like. If anybody'd asked, I woulda said the best bet was upstream, but I'd done been and come up empty. It weren't much of nothing from there to the Tallulah River. If something was in the river, somebody shoulda noticed it already, what with all the tourists and such tromping around out that way.

The brush rustled behind me. I whirled, hand on the 1911 strapped to my hip, and froze. Riley Treadwell stood there big as a bear, dressed in his uniform, sharply pressed green trousers and a black polo with Georgia's Department of Natural Resources logo embroidered on it. My heart sunk clean down to my knees. I knowed I was gonna have to talk to him again sooner or later. I was just counting on it being later, not out in the woods up to my chin in one of Fame's problems.

"Hey, Sunny."

"Riley." I sighed and tromped away from the creek bed. "What you want?"

He jabbed a thumb over his shoulder. "Saw your daddy's car on the side of the road. Figured I'd better check on you in case you'd broke down."

"Mighty kind of you."

"What're you doing out here?"

I glared at him. "Minding my own. How 'bout you?"

"Christ, Sunny. I was worried about you, not trying to catch you red handed." He resettled his DNR ball cap over that nearly red hair of his and glared right back at me. "You ever think about giving people the benefit of the doubt before you jump all over them?"

I snapped my jaws shut over a smart remark. He was

right, for one, though I sure as tootin' weren't gonna tell him the reason I was prickly around him didn't have nothing to do with doubting him. That was a whole nother can of worms, so I held on to my temper. Fame'd found something in the water. If anybody could do something about it, it was Riley.

I fixed something close to an apology on my face. "Anybody complained about the water out this way?"

"Matter of fact, I was on my way to check on it when I saw your car. Fly fisherman called it in. Said he found a slew of dead fish out this way."

"Where at?"

"Up a bit." He pulled off his cap and slapped it on his thigh, and his eyes drifted away from mine. "You hear anything?"

Well, shoot. Couldn't rightly tell Riley why I was looking. He was a lawman, after all, and duty bound to turn in law breakers, even one breaking laws outside his jurisdiction. Still, I kinda needed his help. Sounded like he might need mine a bit, too.

"Seen some dead fish upstream," I finally said. "Water up that way's got a funny sheen to it, kinda like an oily rainbow floating on top."

He nodded. "Fame found something in the water, huh."

I leveled an even stare on him, and he grinned, kinda slow and sly.

"Come on, Sunny. It's not like him making 'shine is a secret. I've had a sip or two myself." He fingered the brim of his hat and slapped it back on. "Rumor has it there'll be some at Jazz and BobbiJean's wedding next month.

'Course there'd be. I was bringing it. "Gossip is a sin, same as lying."

"Like you're not lying to me."

"Not a bit," I said, real cheerful like.

He grunted, though his mouth twisted into a smile. "Rumor has it you'll be there with bells on."

"You been talking to BobbiJean."

"Ran into her and Jazz at Ingles. She mentioned you needed a date. I thought maybe me and you could go together."

I snorted. "Yeah, right. A Carson and a Treadwell going to a shindig together. Our grandpappies'd turn over in their graves."

He crossed them big arms of his over his chest and that smile turned into a smirk. "If I didn't know better, I'd think you were afraid of spending time with me."

"Good thing you know better," I retorted. "You gonna hunt down the problem with the water or jaw me to death?"

"I figured I could do both at the same time," he said mildly. "Come on. You can ride with me."

I stowed up. "I ain'ta doing nothing with you."

His smile dropped in a flash and his face went cold and hard. "Jesus, Sunny, what do you have against me anyway?"

"Not a thing. Don't mean I'm getting in a vehicle with you."

"You wanna help Fame or not?"

I glowered at him. Well, dang. How come he always caught me in a bind? "I'll follow you to the cut off on the other side of the creek. There's a better parking spot out that way. We can ride up together from there."

"Good, then." He held out his hand. "Come on. I'll walk back with you."

I scrubbed my hands against my thighs and stared at that hand.

He waved his fingers, beckoning me closer. "I don't bite."

"I know that."

His hazel eyes flicked down my body and landed on my muddy knees. "If you hold my hand, I can help you keep your balance."

"I been kneeling by the creek side, is all. I ain't fell once."

"Uh-huh." He wiggled his fingers again. "You used to

hold my hand all the time."

"Yeah, when we was kids."

Them hazel eyes of his went all stern like. I heaved a sigh and took his hand. It weren't that big a deal, were it? That's what I told myself, anyhow. Never mind the heat of his skin on mine or the sparks racing up my arm where our palms met.

He twined our fingers together and tugged me closer. "That's my girl."

"I ain't no girl, Riley Treadwell, and I sure as tootin' ain't yourn."

He turned and led me through the woods, swiping tree limbs outta the way and helping me over felled logs like I was a queen or something. "You used to be. Remember?"

"We was kids, what, about eight and eleven?"

He grinned over his shoulder at me. "Yeah, but true love knows no bounds."

I rolled my eyes. "Good grief, Riley. It's a wonder you get any women with them kinda sappy lines."

"Hey, it was the best summer of my life. Swimming in the lake together, making sand castles, endless sunny days."

That weren't quite how I remembered it, like some Norman Rockwell moment captured forever in perfect nostalgia. No, my memories was a bit different, of my mama dropping me off at the swimming beach in the morning with a sandwich and a thing of Kool-Aid. Some days I got to eat that sandwich and some days it was stole before I could get to it. The kids wasn't exactly nice to me. Mostly, they was just indifferent, right up 'til that snake come after Riley and I snatched it outta the water and wrung its dang neck.

I always had quick hands. Snakes never bothered me none, neither, but that'un scared me some good, slicing through the water right toward a boy with a ring of fire for hair what weren't paying no never mind to where he was.

Riley's mama, now, she went on and on like I walked on water or something. Then on, I didn't go hungry and I never had to sit all alone on the beach after ever body went home, waiting on Mama to remember she left me somewhere else.

She weren't a bad mama, just a mite forgetful.

We swished our way through a cluster of ferns and hopped onto the road bank, Riley holding my hand the whole time. I tried tugging on it ever once in a while and he'd tighten his fingers like he didn't mean to let go.

Which was just silly. I was gonna need my hand back sooner or later, weren't I?

He finally let go after opening my car door for me. "Drive careful, Sunny."

I rolled my eyes. "It's a coupla miles. Ain't like I can get lost between here and there."

"No, but you're liable to sneak off on me." He leaned against the car, one arm stretched along the top, the other over the open car door, boxing me in. "Stick with me and I'll treat you to a late lunch in town."

A flutter of nerves hit me, down low where I weren't supposed to look. "Why you keep asking me out?"

"Why do you keep turning me down?" He flicked his fingertip along the tip of my nose and eased back. "See you in a few."

I watched him walk away. Lordy, I knowed it was a sin to lust after a man's rear, but he had a fine'un, he did, nice and firm and, whew. Between that and his broad back and them mile long legs, I was about ready to burst into flames by the time he made it to his work truck, and wouldn't that've been a sight to see?

WE FOLLOWED the pattern set with my wanderings, starting from the place where that fly fisherman reported finding a mess of dead fish. Sure enough, there they was, pooled up against the edges of the creek.

Riley hunkered down and stared at 'em for a long time.

I stood beside him, studying his expression. It was kinda

tight and solemn, and about as serious as I ever seen it. "What's wrong?"

He stood up real slow, never moving his gaze from them fish. "I was just wondering what killed those fish and what we're gonna have to do to get it out of the water."

"We need to find it first, assuming it weren't a onetime thing." I didn't reckon it was. It'd been a few days since Fame tested the water out near us and that sheen was still hanging around. I jerked my head toward upstream. "Get a move on, soldier boy. I ain't got all day to lollygag like you government workers do."

He grinned. "God, Sunny, you're something else. Just for that, you owe me two meals."

I narrowed my eyes at him. "You said you was treating."

Not that I had any intention of going with him, but still. A man asks a woman to dinner, he best be ready to pay.

"I am. Now it's for two meals, though. I figure I stick around you and your smart mouth long enough, we'll be eating together for a week."

"Hardy har, Mr. Funny Man."

He threaded his fingers through mine and started out upstream, following an animal trail winding between the water on our right and the bottom edge of a hill on our left. "You could have pity on me and just agree to go out with me. Then I wouldn't have to keep making up excuses to see you."

That funny flutter started up in my innards again and my breath went all wonky. Had he really been making excuses to see me or was he pulling my leg? "Maybe I just don't like to date."

"Maybe you're just ornery. Call me crazy, but I kinda like that about you." He stopped abruptly and sniffed the air. "You smell that?"

I inhaled and got a big whiff of rotten eggs. Sulfur, sure as tootin'. I grimaced and put my wrist over my nose. "Where's that coming from?"

"Hell if I know." He tugged my hand and pushed me

behind him. "Come around to my other side. I don't want you to accidentally slip into the water."

"I ain't that clumsy," I muttered. "Geez. You been talking to Fame?"

"Not since I was seventeen."

We picked our way more careful like another twenty yards upstream and rounded a sharp bend in the creek. Soon as we did, Riley muttered a string of curses under his breath, too low for me to catch all of 'em. Didn't need to, though. I was kindly thinking the same thing. Up ahead, somebody'd dumped half a dozen waste barrels along the side of the creek. One had fallen over into the water and cracked, probably on one of the rocks lining the creek bed. More'n likely, it was leaking something nasty out into the water.

Looked like we found what was killing the fish and ruining Fame's liquor.

Riley pointed to the steep slope on our left. "Probably dumped from up there."

I nodded. "Road can't be too far from the top of that ridge. Kinda isolated, too."

"Bet whoever dumped it wasn't expecting it to be found."

"Lots of hikers through here, mostly locals."

"Yeah," he agreed. "Those barrels haven't been here long."

"We gonna try to get that'un out?"

His hand tightened on mine, hard as stone, and he rounded on me, his hazel eyes near blazing. "Are you out of your ever loving mind, Sunny? If it's killing the fish, it's probably hazardous."

I shrugged. "I just meant, you know, we *somebody*, not me and you specific like."

He blew out a breath and shook his head. "Environmental Protection Division, maybe. I have to call it in, get somebody out here to test the water, issue an alert for the tourists."

I eyed the barrels. "I bet you got three yards of

paperwork to fill out, too."

"You're not getting out of a meal with me that easy, sweetheart. Damn it." He swept off his cap and swiped it along his thigh. "And we were this close to a real date."

I let my eyes go real wide and pursed my lips, hiding a smile. "I ain't got no intentions of breaking bread with you."

"By golly, if you have to sit on my lap behind my desk, you're eating with me."

He said it without rancor. I knowed he was serious, though, just by the way he held my hand and looked at me with them hazel eyes of his, kinda warm and sweet.

And lordy, I was beginning to like that look about as much as he liked my orneriness.

WE HEADED back to Riley's work truck so he could call them barrels of waste in or whatever it was he done when a mess like the one we stumbled on cropped up. I waited him out a polite distance away, then hopped in his truck so he could carry me back to the IROC.

While we was a-driving, I studied him on the sly. Here we was out on Labor Day weekend and him working. Now me, I didn't make much of a distinction between the days. One was as good as the next, I figured, 'less there was church or something. Riley struck me as the five day workweek, weekends for play kinda guy, not a man what worked on a blue skied Saturday afternoon.

"Why ain't you out enjoying your Labor Day weekend?" I asked kindly outta the blue.

"'Cause that's when folks are liable to break the law." He shifted his hands on the steering wheel and resettled into the driver's seat. "Why are you out working?"

"'Cause that's when it needed doing." I glanced out the passenger's side window, studying the passing scenery. Summer dry woods and thick undergrowth, and fluffy clouds floating above it all. "Something's been bothering me about this whole mess."

He glanced at me, one ginger eyebrow arched. "Just one something?"

"Lots, but this'un kinda particular like. We found them barrels in the wrong waterway."

"What do you mean?"

"I started at the creek near..." I bit my tongue. Couldn't tell Riley where Fame got his liquor water from. Now that woulda been a mess, sure enough. "Let's just say where you found me weren't the first place I looked and call it even."

That slow smile lifted his mouth and went right to his eyes. "Fair enough."

"That weren't nowhere near where we found that junk. The places I looked before you found me was upstream, more'n one. How'd that waste stuff get into them other creeks if the barrels was dumped in a creek what don't even meet 'em 'til downstream?"

He tapped a thumb against the steering wheel and scowled at the road ahead of us. "I'm more worried about why anybody would dump toxic waste into the waterways in the first place. This area depends on tourism."

"Hang the tourists, Riley. Lots of folk still eat the dadgum fish." I orta knowed. I was one of 'em. "You gonna let ever body know?"

"Soon as I can. We'll alert the radio stations and the *Tribune*, pin notices on the information boards around the wilderness areas."

"All right, then." I crossed my arms over my bitty breasts and tried on accommodating for size. He'd helped me out, after all. I reckoned that deserved a reciprocating hand. "You want, I can get the word out."

"You might want to warn Fame, at least, maybe tell him to spread the word."

"I can do that."

The IROC appeared ahead. Riley slowed the truck and flipped on the turn signal. "Now that you've figured out

Fame's problem, you think you might have time to work on Belinda's?"

All the warmth drained outta my day. I tightened my arms around my chest and hunched my shoulders. "I ain't decided."

"I know you were up there, Sunny."

"Is that so?" I shook my head. "I was just seeing what was what."

"Huh."

"Something's wrecking the docks and such out there."

"Yeah."

The placid tone riled me something good. "You know what it is, why don't you fix it?"

"I don't know what it is. Nobody does." He pulled in behind the IROC and parked, then flipped the ignition switch off. "Thing is, you've got a reputation for tracking weird stuff down, have ever since..."

A lump rose in my throat, big as a stump and twice as stubborn. I swallowed it down and nodded. "You can say his name, Riley."

"I don't want to hurt you," he murmured. "You've been through enough."

"I'd say we're about even there."

"Not even close." He cleared his throat and that thumb went to tapping again. "Most of the folks with houses on Greenwood Cove will be at Rhapsody. We could go together. It'd give you a chance to talk to everybody, maybe help you make up your mind."

I dropped my hands into my lap and gawked at him. "You want to take me to Rhapsody?"

"Why not? I've already got the tickets."

"But you want to go with me." Something kinda sick and twisted lodged itself in my gut. Me, backwoods Sunshine Walkingstick, at a society charity function amongst all them fancy folk? I opened the passenger's side door and slid outta the truck, planting both feet on terra firma, right where they belonged. "I don't know what you're playing at Riley, but it ain't funny. I don't appreciate it neither. You go find another woman to make a fool of."

His handsome mug twisted into a scowl. "You know what, Sunny? Sometimes I wonder why I even bother trying with you."

"What's that supposed to mean?"

"Figure it out." He twisted this way and that in the seat as he dug his wallet out, then pulled out a business card and handed it to me. "You change your mind, give me a holler. I'm going anyway. Promised Mama I would."

And Riley Treadwell hadn't never let his mama down, not once. I stuck his card in my pocket. "Tell your mama I said hello."

"Come to Rhapsody and tell her yourself."

"I'll think on it." I jabbed my thumb over my shoulder. "Better run tell Fame what's up."

"I'll let you know if we figure out what's going on. Tell him he might want to stay away from the local water until we do."

I nodded and turned, and got about two paces away from him.

"Sunny?"

I half-turned toward him. "Yeah?"

"You still owe me those meals."

I pivoted toward the IROC, hiding the slow grin spreading across my face. "Keep on dreamin', Riley."

He laughed and raised his voice. "Sometimes that's all a man's got, sweetheart."

I shook my head and got in the IROC. Sure as tootin', if I stayed a minute longer, he'd talk me into something. My heart'd always been a mite too soft where Riley was concerned. It didn't need me helping it along, nor him neither.

5

Soon as I got home, I hightailed it up the trail to Fame's. His car was gone and so was the boys'. I knocked on the door anyhow. Might be one of 'em was still there, and Fame needed to know about the water now, not whenever I could catch him.

Sure enough, the doorknob jiggled and the door opened wide. Missy's voluptuous frame filled the entryway. "Sunny Walkingstick, what are you doing knocking?"

"Didn't know if anybody was home." I sidled in behind her and shut the door tight. "Got news on the water, if Fame's around."

Missy sank into a chair at the kitchen table and tucked her bare feet into the rungs. "He ran into town for me. Should be back soon, if you want to wait."

I slumped into a chair next to her. "Naw. Just let him know to stay away from the water for a while. We found some nasty junk in a couple of the nearby creeks. Don't know if the same stuff is around here, but he don't need to take a chance 'til we can get it cleaned up."

"By *we* you mean...?"

I scowled and glanced away from the curiosity decorating her pretty face. "I run into Riley Treadwell this morning."

"I see."

"You don't got to act so knowing and all." I rolled my shoulders and slid lower in the chair. "Geez, Missy. It ain't like we're dating or nothing."

Heat flared along my cheekbones, burning me sure as fire. Me and my fool mouth. What'd possessed me to mention *dating* and *Riley* in the same sentence, and in front of Missy, no less?

She leaned forward and caught my gaze. "He asked you out."

"Tried to finagle me into eating with him today." I blew out a breath. Well, dang. Now I was gonna have to spill the whole thing, else she'd spend the rest of the day nagging me about it. Like I had time for that. "Said he's got an extra ticket if I wanna go to Rhapsody with him."

Missy blinked twice, shading her violet eyes. "I hope you said yes."

I squirmed on the chair. "Thing is, I kind of accused him of trying to make me into a fool."

"Sunshine Walkingstick," she snapped.

I sat up straight real quick like. "Now, Missy—"

"Don't you *now, Missy* me, young lady." She sucked in a breath and speared me with her *you're in big trouble now* stare. "Riley Treadwell is a decent young man. Don't think I didn't check, because I did, and all I heard were good things."

"I never said he weren't—"

"I'm not finished."

I hunched my shoulders around my ears. "Yes'm."

She nodded once, sharp and fierce, and her wild sable curls bounced around her head. "A decent young man asked you out and you treated him as if he were trying to pull one over on you. What were you thinking?" She held up a finger. "No, don't answer that. I know what you were thinking and I can honestly say this is the first time I've ever been ashamed to call you mine."

The breath whooshed right outta my lungs, leaving my innards hollow and sick. "Missy..."

"You're going out with him."

"But I—"

"Yes, that's exactly what you're going to do. You're going to call him and accept his invitation." A smile started up in her eyes and some of the heat drained outta her voice. "We'll go shopping on Tuesday, as soon as the Labor Day traffic eases up."

I recoiled away from her. "What on Earth do I wanna go shopping for?"

"For a dress, a nice one, and some shoes, too. I've got some money set aside for it. Heaven knows, I've waited long enough to use it." She leaned forward and patted my arm, and a pleased smile bloomed across her face. "This is just what I needed, too. Since my ring went missing, I haven't had a single easy moment. A trip to the mall will be just the thing to take my mind off of it for a while."

I closed my mouth around the uneasiness sinking through me. I hadn't forgot about her ring, not one bit, and I sure didn't have it in me to disappoint her any more. "I'll call him tonight, when he's had a chance to cool off some."

She beamed at me, like I just handed her the winning lottery ticket. "Oh, you'll have so much fun, Sunny. I haven't been to a dance in ages. Maybe I'll get Fame to take me."

I laughed and all the uneasiness dissipated. "I'd pay to see it."

"You wouldn't be the only one." She sighed, a happy sound what sorta floated outta her. "Well, at least one of us will have fun."

I doubted that. Couldn't bring myself to ruin her

enjoyment, though. "He sorta asked me to go with him so I could talk to the folks out on Greenwood Cove. The ones having trouble with their docks and such?"

"I remember. You've decided to help them, then?"

I shook my head. "Still thinking on it. I went out there the other day and poked around some. Met this really gorgeous man, too."

She arched one eyebrow. "Why, Sunshine Walkingstick. You've been holding out on me."

"Not quite," I said drily. "This'un sprung up on Belinda's dock while I was looking it over. Said his name was Abercio Okeanos. Lordy, was he something."

"Abercio Okeanos," she murmured. "That sounds very familiar."

I shrugged. "I never met him before. Don't think he's from around here, neither. Had this really awesome accent. You shoulda seen him, Missy, all dripping wet with nothing but swimming trunks on." Just thinking on it heated my skin up. I shivered and propped my elbows on the table. "And sexy. He kissed my fingers, he really did, and he said something as how he liked the sun shining on the water. I was pretty sure he didn't mean the big, ol' yellow ball in the sky, neither."

Missy's mouth tilted into a frown. "He came on to you."

"Well, it do happen ever once in a while." Not often enough for me to get used to it, more's the pity. "Said he'd see me this Friday and we was gonna..."

"You were going to what?"

"Dance. He said he'd see me Friday and we was gonna dance, but that was before Riley asked me to go to Rhapsody." How had Teus knowed I'd be at Rhapsody when I hadn't knowed it myself? I shook the nonsense outta my head. Nobody could tell the future, could they? 'Cept maybe Old Mother, and she weren't no certainty. "I reckon he figured I was one of Belinda's friends and he'd see me there or something."

"I'm not so certain, Sunny." Missy drew her lower lip between her teeth and gnawed on it. "I don't like the sound of this gentleman at all."

"Oh, poo, Missy. He was just trying to get my goat, is all. You shoulda seen the way he dived back into the water, though, like he was part of it. Didn't even make a splash."

"Didn't..." She grabbed my arm and her fingers dug in real hard. "Tell me everything, Sunny, every single detail."

I shot her a side-eyed look, but I did as she asked, relating ever moment from the time Teus appeared behind me to the time he dove into the water. "I'm telling you, Missy, he weren't harmless, but he was nice enough. Said I could call him Teus and—"

The color leached from her face. "*Teus.* Oh, no. No, no, no."

"What is it, Missy?"

"If this man is who I think he is, he's very dangerous."

My eyebrows shot up. "You know him?"

"Yes. No." She squinched her eyes shut and shook her head, jiggling them sable curls of hers. "Maybe."

I barked out a laugh. "Well, that was clear as mud."

"No, Sunny, please. Listen to me. I think I've met this man before, a long, long time ago, before I came into possession of my ring. He's not what he appears to be." She shook her head again. "No, he's *never* what he appears to be. Don't trust him, sweetie. Don't you dare trust this man."

That was an easy enough promise to make. I didn't hardly trust nobody, let alone a charming, handsome as sin stranger. "I weren't planning on it."

"Good." She sighed and patted my arm right over the bruises she'd dug into it. "Good, then. You'll call Riley tonight?"

"I done said I would."

My words didn't have any starch behind 'em, much as they shoulda. My mind was too caught up on Missy's reaction to Belinda's outlander friend. Me and her visited a while longer, then I trudged on home, worrying over Missy knowing Teus and that dadgum promise she finagled outta me. I was gonna have to call Riley and eat some crow. I hadn't never liked the taste of it, neither.

I PUT IT OFF 'til eight o'clock, like a child avoiding a hated chore. In between, I throwed myself into shining the trailer up good, scrubbing the worn linoleum in the kitchen and the bathroom 'til it sparkled, dusting down all the cobwebs.

No matter how clean a body liked their roost, spiders was determined to muck up the place. Living in the middle of the woods made it twice as hard to keep the dadgum things from crawling inside and planting roots.

I dusted and vacuumed and changed sheets, did the scant two loads of laundry accumulated over the week, not counting the sheets and towels, and finally, I just couldn't put it off no more. I dug Riley's card outta my pocket and dialed his number.

He answered on the third ring. "Hello?"

My mind went about as blank as a clean chalkboard. "Um."

I winced. Oh, lordy, was I an idjit. This was Riley, for crying out loud. I'd knowed him since we was kids. Shoot, I even seen him nekkid once. He was about eleven at the time and scrawny as a bean pole, but still. I seen him in all his natural glory. Why I let him intimidate me now was beyond me.

I took a deep breath and tried again. "It's Sunny."

Something squeaked on his end, and when he spoke, his voice was warm and rich. "I figured you'd torn my card up by now."

If I'da thought on it, I mighta. Too bad for me I spilled my guts to Missy first. "No, I still got it."

"And you used it, too."

"Yeah, I, uh." I winced and cleared my throat. Dang, this

was harder'n I imagined it'd be. "You still want me to go to Rhapsody with you?"

"If you want to go with me."

Not rightly, but I'd already promised, hadn't I? "I reckon I should."

"I'll pick you up on Friday, then. What color dress are you wearing?"

I gripped my cellphone real tight. "Missy's taking me shopping on Tuesday. Won't know 'til then."

"Call me when you know."

My eyes slid closed. Oh, Lordy. I hadn't even made it through the first call, and he already wanted me to call again? Hadn't he talked to me enough in the past week? "Why?"

"So I can pick out something that matches."

"Oh."

"I don't want to wear a brown suit if you're wearing blue."

"Oh."

His soft chuckle tickled my ear. "Ask Missy if a black suit will be ok and what color tie would go best with your dress."

"Maybe you should ask her yourself." I smacked my forehead. Lordy, my mouth had gotten me into a chunk of rudeness here lately. "I mean, maybe I'm not the best person to ask her that."

"I trust you."

Well, that made one person, anyhow. "You ain't gonna try to cash in on them meals, are you?"

"There'll be food there, and no, that doesn't count." That squeak came again and I finally placed it. He was shifting around on something leather, sounded like. "You still owe me two meals. That's two dates."

"I never agreed to the first one," I muttered.

"Give it a chance, Sunny. Maybe you'll like being with me."

I dropped my head back and stared at the water stained ceiling. A long time ago, I'd liked being around him a mite too much. *You're beneath his notice, sugar.* I pushed Belinda's voice outta my head, still clear as a bell after nigh on a decade. "I'll see you on Friday."

"Call me Tuesday when you get home."

"I will."

"G'night, Sunny."

The words were soft and sweet. I said goodnight and hung up. Later, when I was in bed and it was just me and God alone in the dark, I remembered that soft sweetness and fell asleep with it echoing in my head.

6

I spent the whole rest of the weekend stewing and worked myself into the ground trying to stop, starting with the trail between me and Fame. Sunday morning, I hauled out his wheelbarrow and carted wood chips and sawdust from the pile behind his trailer to the trail, spreading it out in thick, smooth piles. Winter'd be on us before we knowed it and that trail got mighty muddy after any kinda weather.

That afternoon, I turned on the radio and piddled around my own trailer, repairing little things, finishing up the week's laundry, and generally running through what energy God give me for that day. I'd just sat down to supper with a dog-eared Louis L'Amour when my phone rung. I checked the caller, thumbed the line open, and said hello to BobbiJean.

"Jazz was on duty at lunch yesterday when a man came in with a ring kinda like the one you're looking for," she said.

I turned my book over on the table, saving my place, and sat straight up. "Ya don't say."

"I had to run to Gainesville yesterday, so I haven't seen it myself yet. Jazz was just telling me about it and I thought I'd better let you know."

"'Preciate it. Y'all open tomorrow?"

"Naw. We're at a show in Atlanta right now or I'd open up for you."

I leaned back in my chair and crossed one ankle over the other. "No big. I reckon it'll wait 'til I can get in there."

"How about Tuesday? We could do lunch, me and you. I'll make Jazz watch the shop so we can have some girl time."

I grinned. Ten to one, girl time with BobbiJean meant wedding talk. I didn't mind none a'tall. It was nice hearing somebody else's plans, 'specially when I had none of my own. "Missy's taking me shopping at the mall on Tuesday. You orta come with us."

She hissed in a breath. "Ooo, Sunny, you are the very devil."

I snickered. As if. "Well, it's all your fault I gotta go anyhow. You might as well come along."

"Now, wait a minute. I ain't done nothing lately."

"You told Riley Treadwell I needed a date for your wedding," I said, tart as a green cherry. "And he took it to mean I needed a date, period. We're going to Rhapsody together."

A clattering bang come through the line. I jerked the phone away from my ear and glared at it. A moment later, a breathless BobbiJean come back on. "Sorry, Sunny. The phone slid right outta my hand. Did you say you're going on a date with the hunky Riley Treadwell?"

"Does Jazz know you're lusting after another man?"

"Oh, posh. He's the hunkiest and he knows it." A low, male drawl sounded on BobbiJean's side and she sighed. "That's right, darling," she murmured. "Nobody compares."

I rolled my eyes. "You wanna go shopping or not?"

"Wanna, definitely. Can y'all meet me at Injun Bob's first thing Tuesday? Y'all can take a gander at the ring before we go."

"Sure thing. I'll let Missy know. Maybe having her ring back'll cheer her up some." Or at least get her mind off my love life. "Tell Jazz I said hello."

"Will do. And Sunny?"

"Yeah?"

"Thanks for letting me tag along."

"Hey, you're saving me from Missy's undivided attention."

She laughed, and a few minutes later, we said our goodbyes and hung up. I finished my supper with a grin on my face, neglecting poor Louis while my mind turned over the upcoming trip to the mall.

MONDAY MORNING brung a spatter of business. Young Billy Kildare phoned and asked me to come down and help him look for his favorite Blue Tick, called Ol' Blue. Dadgum dog run off about ever other week, and poor Billy fretted the whole time, worried something had eat his best friend. Most of the time, it lit off in search of female companionship. Soon as Billy hung up, I called around. Sure enough, Billy's dog had wiggled his way under a fence and had a high ol' time with a lady friend down the road named, appropriately enough, Lady.

The Kildares lived not half a mile from me and Ol' Blue weren't a half mile beyond that. I pulled on sturdy tennis shoes and walked over, picked up the Blue Tick, and dropped him off at Billy's on my way home. As payment, his mama Dori gifted me with enough sour cream pound cake to do me three days, and Billy swore he'd keep a better eye on his dog.

I had my doubts there, but I let 'em pass. Billy was a good young'un, wide eyed and freckle faced, not much older'n Henry woulda been if he'da lived. I couldn't do for Henry no more, but I sure could do for other young'uns. Plus, Dori Kildare had the magic touch where pound cakes was concerned. Only a fool would pass a slice up, and I sure as tootin' weren't no fool.

Harley Jimpson was sitting on the steps of my porch when I come home, his wrinkled face sagging in a forlorn frown. I sighed and invited him in for a glass of sweet tea. Long as Fame and Harley was friendly, I couldn't get outta helping the other man, hang all. Fame was gonna get an earful, though, I sworn, soon as I could pin my uncle down.

I poured Harley some tea and settled into the chair behind my desk, my hand close enough to the .380 for easy pulling. Harley weren't exactly a bad man, but he was slimy as an oil slick and about as trustworthy as a bear with an abscessed tooth.

He sipped his tea and smacked his lips. "Mighty fine tea, Miss Sunny."

"Thank ye kindly. What can I do for you?"

His rheumy eyes took on a canny gleam. "Way I heard it, you was stepping out with the Sheriff's son."

I pressed my lips together. Hadn't taken long a'tall for that rumor to spread and we hadn't been on the first date. "Me and Riley go way back. Don't mean we're stepping out."

"So you wouldn'ta heard none what he's doing snooping around the water."

"Matter of fact, he found what might be toxic waste dumped into the waterways near y'all. You might wanna keep you and yourn outta there for a while."

Harley's lips curled back in a snaggle-toothed grin. "You know an awful lot for somebody he ain't stepping out with."

"We're friends," I said, patient and even like. Friendly, anyhow, and I reckoned that was close enough where Riley was concerned. "You need something else?"

Harley's expression hardened. "Here's your hat, what's your hurry?"

I inched my hand toward the hilt of the .380. "I got business, is all. Fame's expecting me up his way soon. You know how he is about being on time."

"I know Fame right well, little missy, maybe better'n you do." Harley slapped his palms on his thighs and stood. "'Preciate the news."

"Any time. Give your family my regards. Keep 'em outta the water."

"No worries there. Ain't got a one what likes getting wet."

I showed him out and locked the door behind him, and danged if my phone didn't ring as soon as his car's engine turned over. I picked it up and answered, and that was the last I thought on Harley Jimpson for a good, long while.

ME AND MISSY run out to Injun Bob's first thing the next day, me with a wad of nerves filling up my gut, her all wreathed in smiles.

BobbiJean was waiting for us behind the counter wearing a t-shirt over her rooster pants. "I've got breakfast for us. Jazz got up early and made us some fresh biscuits and country ham."

I propped my elbows on the counter and stifled a yawn. Mornings was fine by me. I liked the sunrise same as the next woman, but Missy done drug me outta bed a mite too early. Said we had to hurry or we'd miss all the good stuff in the after Labor Day crowd.

Another yawn sneaked its way out. "You got coffee, too?" I asked.

Missy patted my shoulder. "We'll stop at Micky D's and get all you want, Sunshine."

BobbiJean spun around on her stool and hopped off. "I got that ring in the back. Didn't want it to slip away on us."

She headed into the office and was back out again before I could hardly blink. She slid a tiny plastic bag across the counter. Missy picked it up and held it in the flat of her palm, shaking her head.

I blinked through the grit filling my eyes and grunted. The ring was gold, all right, and had an inset ruby, and it was shaped kinda like Missy's, but it weren't hers.

BobbiJean's shoulders slumped. "Well, shoot. I'm sorry, Missy."

"It's close, BobbiJean, so very close." Missy's lips trembled into a wobbly smile. "Thank you for letting us look."

I straightened and covered Missy's hands with my own. "It'll turn up, Missy. You wait and see."

"It has to, Sunny," she said, and her voice was all wrong, so sad and hoarse and frail, and for a minute, that strange sense come to me, of fresh mowed grass and a musty tomb and the hot stench of the dying.

I shook it off and led her and BobbiJean out to the IROC. We backtracked to Micky D's, ordered a ton of coffee, and ate Jazz's from-scratch country ham biscuits as we roared down the highway. By the time we hit the Mall of Georgia, Missy was near back to her old self again.

More's the pity.

Them two gals could shop like demons. We run into and out of ever shop in the whole dadgum place, those what had fancy dresses. I tried on enough for a whole army of women, short dresses, long dresses, dresses with sleeves and them without, and some held up by nothing a'tall.

How was a woman supposed to keep her boobs covered in a dress like that anyhow?

The three of us finally agreed on a cranberry colored, scoop necked satin dress with cap sleeves and a mid-thigh hem. That's what BobbiJean called it, anyhow. Me? I just called it a red dress.

Missy picked me out some shoes, and there again, the two of 'em went all fancy on me. Shoes was shoes, wasn't they? These was mighty fine and they suited the dress and my scrawny legs ok, but they was just shoes. After that come matching underwear and hose, and I'd about had enough by the time we was done in the lingerie store.

While we was at it, Missy made me buy a good, winter coat. It was black wool, nice and thick, and fell below my hiney, so at least I wouldn't freeze. And then, Lord help me, we had to match the dress to a tie. My cheeks burned something fierce the whole time. Imagine, having to buy a man a tie so his outfit wouldn't clash with mine.

I held up the one Missy picked out, squinting at the sedate texture swirling through the solid dark red, the same color as my dress. Cranberry, BobbiJean said. Riley's hair weren't so red the tie would look funny. Fact was, I figured he'd look fine no matter what he wore, which sorta made the whole fuss to find the perfect tie nothing but a big bother.

BobbiJean and Missy picked out plenty of their own stuff 'long and along. We shopped right through lunch, then loaded all our bags in the trunk of the IROC and ate at the Macaroni Grill. I drove home with the radio on low so I could listen to their excited chatter about savings and sales and, oh, wouldn't Sunny and Riley make the perfect couple?

I snorted and played grumpy, but later that night, after I called Riley and told him about the tie, I hung that dress up where I could look at it and climbed into bed thinking on how even a woman like me felt beautiful in a dress like that.

7

Riley knocked on my door at six sharp on Friday evening.

I smoothed my hands down my dress over the butterflies flapping in my stomach. Missy'd come over and done up my hair, pinning it on top of my head with two straight sticks. She let me borrow some of her jewelry, too, a heavy gold choker and a matching bracelet, and she painted my face so I felt more like a doll than a living, breathing woman.

"Sunny?" Riley called. "You ok?"

I snatched open the door, and ever thought in my head drained right out. Riley was wearing a black suit what looked like it was handmade just for him. His shoulders seemed somehow wider in it, his hips more narrow. He'd left the collar of his shirt unbuttoned, a plain white shirt over a plain white undershirt, and he'd shaved and done something to his hair so it had a little wave to it.

He smiled, slow and easy. "You look beautiful."

"Ah. Hmm." Him, too, though danged if I'd tell him. Didn't want him getting no ideas. I stepped back and let him in, then shut the door. "I got your tie in the back. Missy fixed it for you."

I turned real careful like. Dadgum shoes. I'd practiced walking in 'em all week. Thank goodness Missy'd found some with decent heels instead of them spiky things most ever body else favored. "Come on back. You can use my bathroom to fix your tie."

He followed me into the bedroom, slipped on the tie, and adjusted it using the mirror over the bathroom sink. "This has to be the cleanest bathroom I've ever seen."

"It'll be your last look, so take your fill."

He grinned and fastened a gold tiepin to his tie and shirt. "I'm aiming for it to be the first of many."

I rolled my eyes. "Keep on dreamin', Riley."

"You know what I'm gonna say." He buttoned his coat over his tie. "There. How's that?"

"Fit for a king. Can we go now?"

"You in a hurry to get there?"

"In a hurry to get it over with," I retorted. "Shake a leg."

"One more thing." He eased up to me and settled his hands on my waist. "Perfect fit."

I rested my hands on his shoulders, more for balance than anything. Leastwise, that's what I told myself. Holding on to his solid strength didn't have a thing to do with it. "What's a perfect fit?"

"Me and you, exactly the way I thought we'd be." His eyes dropped to my mouth, and he leaned down and brushed his cheek along mine. "Tonight after we eat and dance and talk to everybody in God's creation, I'm gonna bring you home and find out if you taste as good as you look."

Them butterflies multiplied, filling me from stem to stern. I hitched in a breath and clutched his shoulders. His aftershave tickled my nose, sharp and masculine, the headiest thing I ever smelled. His hands tightened on my waist, and I sworn, I could feel ever inch of him where he touched me.

"Think about that while you're dancing with other men tonight, Sunny. Think about how I'm gonna kiss you."

His breath feathered across my ear, leaving delicious shivers of heat in its wake, and I bit back a moan. Ten to one, I wouldn't think on nothing else the whole night long.

RHAPSODY IN RABUN was an annual bash put on by the muckity mucks as a way to salvage their consciences for having more than other folk, about like ever other charity, I figured. The proceeds from this year's event was earmarked for the local women's shelter. It was a good enough cause, though I'da rather done anything else to support it 'sides mingle with folks I didn't know and, truth be told, didn't wanna know.

Riley placed his hand low on my back and left it there as he guided me through the crowd, warming me through my dress. For some odd reason, having his hand there made me feel like a real lady, safe, protected, beautiful.

Jazz and BobbiJean was the first people we passed what weren't strangers. He had on a baby blue tux with a matching ruffled shirt, and mighta looked like anybody else there 'cept for the musical notes painted up one side of his pants and down the other. She was wearing a yellow chiffon dress we found at the mall and had such a tight grip on Jazz's hand, her knuckles was white.

At least I weren't the only uncomfortable body there.

I pressed my cheek to hers and worked up a good smile for her while our dates shook hands and made man noises. "If you was any prettier, you'd outshine the sun."

She beamed a smile at me. "Thanks, Sunny. I can't believe you're really here."

"Neither can I," I muttered.

Riley rubbed small circles along my lower back. "We need to mingle. Maybe we can meet up with y'all later."

Jazz nodded. "Sure thing, man. I got some hooch out in the truck."

"Yeah?" Riley glanced down at me. "You bring your driver's license?"

"You really gonna sneak outside and sip 'shine with Jazz?" I asked.

Jazz winked at me. "Millard Willoughby's finest."

"The good stuff," Riley said. "They don't allow it in here."

I clucked my tongue. "And you call yourself a lawman."

"Only when I'm at work. C'mon. Belinda's waving at us."

I bit back a retort. She was the whole reason I was there, her and her blasted dock. I promised BobbiJean I'd talk to her later, then Riley led me through the crowd toward where his ex was holding court next to her husband and a handful of people I never seen before.

Belinda Arrowood, née Heaton, had the kind of figure women in the '50s envied and she showcased it about the same way. Last time I seen her, her hair was near about red as a fire truck. Tonight, it was Marilyn Monroe blonde and arranged in careful curls around her dimpled face. She'd squeezed herself into a white, satin cocktail dress and paired it with a truly horrendous, chunky turquoise and gold necklace. Danged if she hadn't painted a beauty mark on her face, too.

Way I figured it, Marilyn was the real thing. Belinda was just a cheap knockoff.

My lips twitched, spite of my intentions. I was s'posed to behave. Reckoned that included thinking kindly on her for the next coupla hours.

We drew near just as Tom slipped away, likely looking for the nearest liquor. I tutted under my breath. Poor Tom. If I was married to that ol' she cat, I'd be an alcoholic, too.

Belinda held out her hand, a queen expecting her due. "There you are, Riley. I was beginning to think you'd skipped out on us."

Riley touched his fingers lightly to hers, then stuck his

hand in his pants pocket. "Nice crowd tonight."

She smiled, flashing her dimples. "We aim to please. Do you know everyone?"

Riley nodded. "Sunny, this is Faith Renault and her friend, Christian Mears."

Faith was a thin woman with a sharp, prominent nose in an ageless face. Her hair was pulled into a severe chignon and her plum colored dress was elegant and a mite too conservative. Christian had to be younger'n her by a decade, maybe a decade and a half given the sour pucker of her lips. He was tall and broad and pretty boy handsome, and his stomach was flat enough under his tailored suit to suggest he was a devotee of the physical.

I lifted a hand from the knot I'd tangled mine into, aiming for friendly, and was pretty sure I missed by a mile.

Riley nodded at two gentlemen standing on the other side of Christian. "And this is Gregory Hightower and his companion, David Eckstrom."

I weren't so dumb I didn't know what companion meant, and it was a right shame both of 'em leaned that way. Gregory was maybe forty and nearly as tall as Riley, though he was leaner with his muscle. He was handsome, too, with even features and a square chin and the prettiest mocha skin I ever seen. David was shorter, maybe five ten, and whipcord thin. He flashed a roguish grin my way, and danged if heat didn't creep up my cheeks.

Men always done that to me, even if they was gay.

"Y'all, this is Sunny Walkingstick, a local investigator," Riley said.

"Little Sunny is good at sorting things out." Belinda's big, blue eyes flashed. She tilted her glass toward me. "Isn't that right, Sunny?"

"I'm good at hunting down what needs to be dealt with," I said evenly. I reckoned nobody needed to hear how I dealt with things, 'specially since it usually involved my daddy's knife and a lotta spilt blood. "I hear y'all got a problem in the cove."

"Not a problem so much as damage from an unknown source," Faith said, her tone stiff as her ramrod straight posture. "What are your qualifications, Ms. Walkingstick?"

I glanced sideways at Riley. "I got references, you need 'em."

"That would be prudent." Faith opened the clasp of her matching clutch and pulled out a business card. "I'm returning to Atlanta tonight. Please feel free to contact me at work or drop by our home on the lake. Christian will be there for a few days more."

I took the card, weighing it in my hand, and run a thumb over the smooth, heavy linen paper. *Faith Renault, CFO, Southern Energies LLC.* Her phone number and e-mail address was under that. "Thank ye kindly."

She nodded once, like she'd fully expected nothing less outta me. "Of course. If you'll excuse us, I promised Christian a dance."

They moved off together, her arm through his, him towering over her slighter form.

David stepped into her place next to Belinda, facing me. "Speaking of dancing. Do you mind if I steal her away for a dance or two, Riley?"

Riley's hand pushed me slightly forward. "I need to find my parents and say hello, anyway."

"Oh, uh." I swallowed hard and shook my head. "Maybe you should dance with somebody else, Mr. Eckstrom. I ain't exactly graceful."

Which weren't a lie, though it weren't the whole truth, neither. I hadn't never danced with nobody before, 'cept when my daddy used to put on one of his old LPs and whirl me around. 'Course, I was just a young'un then. Didn't hardly count none.

David covered my icy hands with his tanned ones. His palms was rougher than I woulda expected and warm. "I'll be gentle."

Gregory's head lowered, not before I caught a quick smile. David turned to him and kissed him smack on the mouth. "You're next, lover."

"If you insist," Gregory said, and I sighed. He had the nicest voice, all low and smooth and sexy.

David slipped one of my hands through his elbow and led me toward the couples dancing in time to the band's '40s-era swing. "I've known Riley for years now and not once did he hint about having you stashed away."

"I weren't hardly stashed away, Mr. Eckstrom."

"David, please. You and I are going to be good friends, Sunny."

I eyed his assured smile. "You reckon?"

"Absolutely." His smile widened, deepening the grooves around his mouth, and his eyes crinkled at the corners as he swung me out onto the dance floor. "You look like a woman who needs to be fed."

So much for being friends. I eased away from him, putting a scant six inches between his flat belly and mine. "I eat."

"What a coincidence? I cook." His hand tightened on my waist. "As a matter of fact, I'm throwing a dinner party in two weeks. Small, intimate. Fabulous food."

My upper lip curled into a sneer. "Not them little fancy do-dads with shrimp and liver, is it?"

He threw his head back and laughed, and his hazel eyes sparkled. "Oh, God, you're adorable. No wonder Riley's hidden you away."

"Weren't no hiding, Mr. Eckstrom. We just ain't got no call to speak to one another much, is all."

"You're not dating him?"

I snorted out a laugh. "Not hardly."

He eased me closer and lowered his voice. "Then you should definitely call me David."

His cheek brushed along mine. In my heels, I was nearly as tall as him and a whole lot more awkward. I concentrated on keeping my steps small and not stepping all over his toes. Never mind the embarrassment. His shoes was too nice to ruin with my clumsiness.

"Mr. David, sir, I know you're gay'n all, but maybe we ortn't dance so close."

He pulled back and met my gaze evenly. "Does my sexuality bother you?"

My eyelids fluttered closed and my cheeks went hot as an open flame. Lordy, I done stuck my foot right into it. "No, sir. It's just, Mr. Hightower seems like a nice man. He probably don't appreciate a woman horning in on his partner."

"Ah. No worries, darling. We have an open relationship."

"But you're gay, right?"

"I like men," he murmured.

I heaved out a relieved breath and quit trying to put a decent distance between the two of us. "I reckon it's ok then."

He huffed out a laugh. "Do you give Riley such a hard time?"

"Naw. I reserve a special kinda hard for him."

"I bet you do."

He whirled me around again in a quick circle, and my heart jumped into my throat. I laughed and clutched his shoulder and nearly tripped over my own two feet. "Not so fast. I ain't used to wearing heels."

"What do you normally wear?"

"Boots. You usually wear the spit and polish?"

"I prefer comfort. Bare feet, worn jeans."

"A man after my own heart."

"Didn't I say we'd be friends?" he said mildly. "You're an investigator?"

"Of a sort," I hedged. "I look into stuff the police ain't no good for."

"Like who vandalized our dock. The police were less than useless."

"They can't solve ever thing, Mr. David. You wasn't up

here when it happened, was you?"

"I was in Atlanta at our apartment. Gregory was out of town at a conference. Tax law." He shuddered. "Deadly dull, if you ask me."

I hid a grin in his shoulder. "How long was you gone before you noticed it?"

"Hmm. Two weeks, maybe? I'd have to look at my calendar to be sure."

"You keep stuff like that in a calendar?"

"You don't?" He turned his face into my throat and sorta hummed. "I just had a fabulous idea. Why don't you come over this weekend and I'll show you my calendar."

I snickered. He might as well have said he wanted to show me his artwork. "If you liked women, I'd think you was coming on to me."

"Who says I wasn't?" The smile in his voice was sweet as sugar. "We can take the motorcycle out, tour the lake, eat on the veranda overlooking the water and all the snotty, second homes."

"I seen enough of 'em, thanks. Maybe I can swing by and have a look-see at your calendar, though, if that's ok."

"It's a date." He sighed and his breath feathered over my skin. "Speaking of, yours for the evening looks like he wants to throttle one of us."

"Probably me. I reckon he wants a dance." Riley's earlier words flitted through my mind and I shivered. Reckoned he wanted more'n a dance. I was tempted, sure I was, but I weren't stupid neither. "I appreciate you being kind'n all. That was my first ever growed up dance."

He stepped back, head tilted to the side, and eyed me from beneath thick, curly eyelashes. "Was it really?"

I flicked a fingertip in a crisscross over my heart. "Wouldn't lie about it."

He dropped my hand and cupped my face in his warm, elegant hands. "I'll savor being your first, darling girl. And for another first."

He dipped his head and kissed me lightly on the mouth, a simple touch, over before I could think on it. I touched my fingers to my lips and gaped at him. "What'd you do that for?"

"I was betting you'd never been kissed by a non-heterosexual man." He tugged me off the dance floor, safely outta the way of couples attempting a swirly dance I didn't recognize. "Two firsts in one night, and mine to claim."

I'd had more'n them two firsts that night, though I weren't rightly gonna tell him that. "You're an odd duck, Mr. David."

"I have a feeling I'm in good company, Sunny."

Riley pushed his way around a knot of people clustered on the edge of the dance floor and scowled at David. "Gregory's looking for you."

David smiled faintly. "Of course. Thank you for the dance, Sunny. Call me this week and we'll set up that date. We're in the book."

I mustered up a smile for him. "Talk to you then."

Riley slid his hand into mine as David slipped through the crowd. "Have a nice chat?"

"I had fun. He writ down ever thing in his calendar. Said I could look at it, if I was of a mind."

"Did he, now." Riley's mouth thinned into a straight slash across his face. "Mama wanted to say hello."

"I ain't seen your mama in a coon's age."

"You could drop by anytime."

Not with his daddy the Sheriff around. I pinned that thought behind my lips and kept my own counsel. Riley'd gone to a lotta trouble to make tonight special for me, and while I weren't too keen on hanging so tight with him, it wouldn't kill me to show a little appreciation.

MY POOR DOGGIES sure got a good workout that night. Riley claimed me about ever other dance, and eventually, I relaxed enough around him to have fun.

I danced with Gregory, and lordy, was he a charmer. Shy and sweet, he was, and so dadgum cute, I was tempted to pinch his cheeks. He filled me in on what he knowed about the damage to the property on Greenwood Cove, which weren't much more'n what David done told me. I asked Gregory about the cove's other property owners. Turned out that of the other two, one had died recently, leaving ever thing to his children, and the other was outta town on vacation. I thanked him proper like and, when he asked, promised I'd do my best to make it to his and David's upcoming dinner party.

Christian asked me to dance, though I figured it was more 'cause Faith prodded him into it. Bless him, for having a face what looked like it was sculpted by Michelangelo, he was a few turnips shy of a full set of smarts. He didn't know a dadgum thing about the problems in the cove, though he was more than willing to talk fashion, weightlifting, and the importance of protein to building muscle.

David horned in on another dance and give me his business card, and after, me and BobbiJean had a high ol' time swinging each other 'round the dance floor while our menfolk slipped outside and snuck some hooch.

They come back in half an hour later, Riley so loose I expected him to melt into a heap on the hardwood floor. He threw an arm around my shoulders and tugged me into a tight hug.

"You drunk?" I asked, my voice muffled by his tie.

"Not even close, sweetheart."

"You sure? 'Cause you seem a mite too happy."

"It's the company." He run his hands down my back and up again, over and over, real slow and easy like. "You having a good time?"

I smiled and clutched his waist through his suit jacket. "I'm having a blast."

"You sound surprised."

"Yeah, maybe. I ain't used to being around so many strangers, but the dancing sure is a lotta fun."

"Give me five and we'll head out again."

"You need help?"

He snickered. "Worried I'm really drunk?"

"You was drinking Millard Willoughby's finest. It's a mite stronger'n Fame's, way I hear tell."

"I swear I'm fine. Here." He dug in his pocket and pulled out his keys. "You can drive us home."

I cupped my hand over the keys. "Ain't got nowhere to put 'em. You get outta hand, though, and me and BobbiJean is gonna strip search you for them keys."

"It's a deal." He smacked a kiss to my forehead. "Be back in a minute."

"Take your time."

I watched him walk away, and danged if he didn't hold to a straight line. Reckon he weren't drunk, then. I puzzled over it a minute, torn between disappointment and relief. It mighta been fun trying to get his keys away from him, 'specially since he stuck 'em back in his pants pocket.

Warm hands cupped my shoulders. I jerked around and run smack dab into Teus. My eyes went round as saucers. I done forgot all about him. "Hey, Mr. Teus."

"Just Teus." He rubbed his hands along my upper arms. "You promised me a dance."

I backed hastily away. "Whoa, now, I never done it. You was the one talking about dancing, not me."

"Don't you want to know what's happening in the cove?"

I narrowed my eyes at him, not trusting them innocent aqua colored eyes of his one bit. "What makes you think I'm interested?"

"You were there, inspecting the area." He shrugged and reeled me back in, bumping my body into his. "Belinda mentioned your name."

I laid my hands flat against his chest and pushed, what good it did me. He held me firm and entirely too close. I was getting a little tired of men doing that to me. Riley was one thing. He was my date, after all. And David, well, he was a big, ol' flirt, but mostly harmless, far as I could tell. Teus was a different kettle of fish. Missy done warned me away from him, and I was inclined to take her advice, what with her being older and more worldly and hopefully a dang sight wiser.

I shoved his chest again. "Let me go right this instant, you gollywhoppin' cretin."

"After we dance."

One of his hands slid down my arm and captured my hand. I give in and tagged along after him toward the dance floor. Tired doggies or not, Teus might know something. I was duty bound to find out what, at least 'til I decided whether I was gonna help Belinda or not.

At the edge of the dance floor, he said, "Do you know the Foxtrot?"

Mischief reared its wicked head inside me. "Is that kinda like a dog trot?"

He slid a side-eyed glance at me. "Sunshine."

"Oh, all right." I sighed and eyed the couples dancing across the floor. "I ain't much on dancing. Tonight was my first night, mostly."

"We'll stick to the box step. Follow my lead?"

I rolled my eyes. "Like I got a choice."

"Graciousness is a virtue, Sunshine." He led me onto the dance floor and positioned us in what I was beginning to think of as the standard dance form, one hand on my waist, the other holding mine in the air, and my free hand on his shoulder. "Watch my feet and mirror my steps."

I did, stepping back when he stepped forward, then to the side, and so on, and pretty soon, I got where I didn't have to look at his feet no more. "That weren't so bad."

"Dance is an art form everyone should master, even young investigators living in the middle of rural America."

"You sound kinda snotty when you say stuff like that."

"I'm merely lamenting the lack of social grace among the

modern generations. Today's young people have no appreciation for the subtlety needed to properly navigate the world."

I narrowed my eyes on his tanned face. "You're insulting me."

"Not you in particular, Sunshine. Your generation in general." He smiled, slow and sensual, and eased me a fraction closer. "I'd be happy to serve as your tutor."

"I got enough men in my life right now, thank ye." Boy, did I ever. Way I figured it, I needed to get a handle on Riley before I stepped out with another man, and I weren't even dating him. "What can you tell me about what's going on in Greenwood Cove?"

"Very little, I'm afraid. My business dealings with the Greenwood Five don't include what happens to their personal property."

I stopped dead in my tracks. "The Greenwood Five?"

"The property owners, or rather, their managers." Teus nudged me back into the dance. "Belinda on behalf of her husband, Gregory on behalf of his."

"Gregory and David ain't married," I pointed out.

Teus smiled. "Faith handles her own dealings, of course. She's a shrewd negotiator."

That was probably the kindest thing anybody done said about her recently. I was sure she'd take it as a compliment, too, and almost sure Teus'd meant it as one. "What about the other two?"

"Hal Woodrow takes care of his own business, now that he's retired. Phillip Oliver has handled his father's estate since Thaddeus died last year." Teus tutted and shook that regal head of his. "A shame, really. The elder Oliver slipped and fell into the lake, hitting his head against the side of his boat on the way in. He drowned before anyone could reach him. Didn't you hear?"

I had the feeling Teus was mocking the late Mr. Oliver somehow, though I couldn't pin down exactly how. "I don't take the paper."

"A situation we'll have to remedy." He whirled me around in a circle. "How attached are you to Mr. Treadwell?"

"Er, he's my date."

"I'm rather aware of that, Sunshine."

"Well, it's the truth." I shrugged and twisted my mouth into a thoughtful frown. "I reckon most people'd call us friends. We've knowed each other since we was kids."

His eyes went dreamy for a minute, then sharpened. "The two of you used to swim together in the lake."

"How did you know?"

"I have my ways," he murmured. "He's headed this way. If you'd rather, I can escort you home."

Missy's warning drifted through my head and I stiffened. "Thank ye kindly, Mr. Teus, but Riley brung me. I reckon he orta be the man to carry me home."

"I'll leave you in his capable hands, then." Teus led me off the dance floor, raised my hand to his mouth, and kissed me lightly on the knuckles. "We'll meet again, Sunshine Walkingstick, sooner than you'd like."

He bowed and backed away, and a minute later, he was lost in the crowd. I stared at the spot where he disappeared, pondering the many things I learned during that one dance, and the many more tidbits I was sure to find once I give it a good thinking over.

8

Rhapsody eventually wound down, thank goodness. I never made it to the silent auction. A shame, too. Jazz and BobbiJean both donated artwork, the folksy stuff muckity mucks raved about. I brung money for it, too, just in case, and then got sidetracked with all the dancing and eating and investigating.

I snuggled under Riley's jacket in the front seat of his Range Rover. My own jacket was in the backseat going to waste, like the tie he yanked off soon as we got in the car. I didn't mind so much. His aftershave had rubbed off on his jacket collar. Having it under my nose the whole drive home seemed like a small price to pay for allowing him to cover me with it.

Nigh on forty-five minutes after we left the Civic Center, Riley parked beside my shabby little trailer and walked me to the door. He skimmed the backs of his fingers along my cheek. "Thanks for going with me."

"Thanks for taking me. I had fun."

"I'm glad." His fingers slid down the side of my neck and toyed with my necklace. "Go out with me again, a real date this time, just me and you. We could go to the movies, maybe have dinner."

Some of the night's pleasantness drained away. "Riley, I..."

He ducked his head and pressed his mouth to mine, stunning me into silence. He drew back almost as quick as he kissed me, though his mouth hovered close to mine. "I know what you're gonna say, and you can forget it. You really think I care about that feud between Fame and my dad?"

"I think you orta."

"Fuck that, Sunny. They can sort out their own problems." He wrapped his hand around my nape. One thumb strummed over my pulse, steady and gentle, stirring heat in my blood. "One date, that's all I'm asking for. You can try it on for size and if you don't like it, I'll quit hounding you about it."

I snorted out a laugh. No, he wouldn't. I knowed better'n that. Still, temptation burned in me, likely helped along by the need whirling along my skin, deep down in my bones, and ever where in between. "Do I gotta wear makeup?"

"Not on my account."

He dipped his head again and nipped the side of my neck, and my skin tingled and burned under his touch. I gasped and closed my eyes and rested my hands on his chest. "Riley, what're you doing?"

"Keeping my promise."

"I don't..." I squeezed my eyes tighter shut. "What promise?"

"To see how you taste," he murmured. "And you taste so good, Sunshine, so beautiful."

His hand tightened on my nape and his mouth came

down on mine, hard and needy, and Lord help me, I opened for him, letting him take whatever he wanted. He devoured me, learning ever bit of my mouth inside and out, and all I could do was cling to him like he was the only thing holding me upright.

Maybe he was.

One kiss become two, merging into an endless series of soft murmurs and desperate gasps. When Riley finally broke away from me, my back was against the side of the trailer, his hand was on my hind end, and my hands was up under his shirt, stroking the bare skin of his stomach. I jerked 'em out and hid my face in his chest right over his thudding heartbeat. "Sorry."

"For what? God, Sunny." His mouth found my pulse and sucked lightly, and my knees went weak again. "Invite me in."

Bad idea. Really bad idea. Me and Riley inside my trailer, both of us het up from that kiss, and a bed a short hallway away? We'd wind up there, sure as tootin', and much as I wanted him, much as I'd always wanted him, I couldn't do it. Fame'd kill one of us, if Riley's daddy didn't do the job first.

"Maybe we should try that date first," I said.

He laughed, husky and short. "Only if it can be soon."

"No sex."

"I'm not promising that."

I rubbed my cheek over his chest. His muscles was firm under his shirt, and so very, very tempting. I sighed and amended my proclamation. "Maybe a kiss or two, then."

"You drive a hard bargain, Sunny, but if that's the only way I can get you to go out with me, I'll take it. How about Sunday?"

I didn't even pretend to think it over. "Sunday's good."

"Then Sunday it is." He eased away from me, pulling me along with him, and wrapped his arms around me. "Can I call you tomorrow when I get off work?"

I bit back a smile. "Lordy, Riley, you're bad as a kid."

"I'm as randy as a kid," he said drily. "Let me get your coat and see you inside."

He bounded down the steps and retrieved my jacket, then waited while I opened up and stepped into the trailer. I shrugged his jacket off and exchanged it for mine. "I really did have fun tonight."

"Me, too." He bent down and pressed his mouth to mine a final time, lingering there for a long, gentle moment before letting me go. "Sleep tight, Sunshine."

"You, too."

I leaned against the doorframe and watched him leave, waved goodbye as he pulled outta my yard, then shut the door, grinning like a loon the whole time. Maybe dating Riley was a bad idea. Lord knowed he irritated me something fierce from time to time, but maybe we could work our way around to friendship again, the way we had when we was young'uns and didn't know nothing outside our own little worlds.

A yawn caught me by surprise, reminding me of the late hour. I slipped off my shoes, hung up my dress, and got ready for bed, replaying that kiss over and over in my head 'til sleep swooped down and claimed me.

A HARD, RAPID KNOCK on my front door woke me early the next morning. I groaned and stumbled outta bed and yanked the door open on a smiling Missy. She held up a cup of coffee in one hand and what looked like a biscuit wrapped in a paper towel in the other. "I'm sorry, Sunny, but I just couldn't wait any longer to hear about your date."

I yawned and shuffled back, inviting her in with a wave of one hand. "It's ok, Missy. I need to get up anyhow."

"Not after a late night, surely." She set the biscuit and coffee down on my desk and sank gracefully into the chair in front of it. "So, tell me everything and don't leave out a single detail."

I slumped into my own chair and blinked at the coffee. "Belinda Heaton's still fake as a three dollar bill. Poor Tom was slushed before the night was half over, bless him."

"Honey, that's business as usual. What about you and Riley?"

My cheeks heated and that sloppy grin slapped itself on my face. "You remember when we was talking about him? You know, the day he come by and asked me about working for Belinda?"

"I remember you telling me he liked it slow and easy."

"Boy, was I ever right."

Her violet eyes rounded. "You slept with him."

"Not hardly, but that goodnight kiss." I sighed and snuggled into the chair. "Lordy, Missy. He had me so hot, I was about crawling all over him. Had my hands up his shirt and ever thing."

"No."

"Oh, yeah. It was plum embarrassing, truth be told. Course, he had his hand on my butt."

"And you didn't punch him?" She sat back and clucked her tongue. "Either you're getting soft in your old age or you really like him."

I closed my eyes, hiding the truth as best I could.

"Oh, Sunny, you sweet girl, you."

My eyes popped open. "Now, don't you go feeling sorry for me, Missy."

"I'm not, truly. Why didn't you tell me?"

I lifted my hands, then let 'em flop into my lap. "There's too much bad blood between our families, and too much history between me and him. 'Sides, I ain't his normal type, not by a long shot."

Missy's lips pursed into a little moue. "You're a good person."

"We gonna go over that dry ground again?"

"Until you get it through your stubborn head." She huffed out a sigh and speared me with a no-nonsense glare.

"You're going out with him again."

"Sunday, to the movies and maybe dinner." Her eyes narrowed, and I held up my hands again. "I couldn't hardly turn him down after that kiss, could I?"

"There was more to it than a kiss, I bet."

"Well, we had a high ol' time at Rhapsody and he was kinda easy to be around, you know? I figured we'd snipe and bicker, but it was...good. Comfortable, even, almost like when we was kids." My memories of that time might've been different than Riley's, but they was still good'uns, mostly so anyhow, right up 'til he hit high school and fell in with the snotty crowd. After that, ever thing changed, just ever thing. "He gets along well with BobbiJean and Jazz, too. Fact is, him and Jazz snuck outside and had some hooch together, and Riley come back in smiling so big, I thought he was snookered."

I started at the beginning and told her the whole tale of my big night out, from the time we got there to the time we come home, and I described ever thing, the food and the band, meeting the folks with houses out on Greenwood Cove. She was mighty curious about 'em, too, so I included ever detail I could remember. Faith's snootiness, Christian's empty head, bless him, Gregory's shy wit, and flirty David with his easy smile and abundance of charm.

"David's having a fancy get together at their house in a coupla weeks, said I was to come out." I threaded my fingers together over my belly. "I'm s'posed to call him next week and meet up with him. He offered to take me on a motorcycle ride. Can you believe that?"

"Are you going to go with him?"

I snorted. "I'm crazy, Missy, not stupid."

"Well, I'm sure he meant well. He sounds like such a nice young man."

"That's the way he struck me." I eyed her glum expression and tapped a thumb against my stomach. "You ok?"

"What? Oh, of course." Her mouth twisted into a slight frown. "I just realized Fame and I haven't been on a date in a long time."

"You tell him you wanna go out, he'll take you wherever you wanna go."

"Perhaps." She shook her head a mite, wobbling the curls piled on top of her head, and smiled. "With all the investigating you're doing, I have to assume you've decided to take on Belinda's case."

"Not yet. There's something there I can't quite pin down."

I sighed and fixed my gaze on the ceiling above her head. One of them things I was uneasy about was Teus. Since Missy'd warned me to stay away from him, I didn't feel right telling her about that dance. I sure didn't wanna share my suspicions about him having more to do with what was going on in the cove than he let on.

"I'll think on it some more, maybe poke around a little. I don't know. Don't seem like there's much of a rush. Leastwise, nobody seemed right anxious about it." Ticked off, yeah. Eager to figure out the problem, not so much. "Say, did I tell you about the getup Belinda was wearing?"

Missy relaxed under my description of the God awful way Belinda'd gommed herself up, and I only exaggerated a little in the telling. By the time she left, I'd worked my way through the bacon biscuit and coffee she brung me, and her smile was firmly in place once more.

A day without Missy's smile was a sorry day indeed. That thought kept a smile on my own mug right up 'til suppertime.

9

Riley called about five minutes after I sat down to supper with a reheated plate of leftovers. I pushed 'em away with nary a regret and answered my phone.

"Hey, Sunny." His yawn drifted through the phone. "Sorry. Didn't sleep much last night."

I smiled and dug the toe of my boot into the carpet, and spun my chair around. "Too much of Millard Willoughby's 'shine?"

"Not enough of Sunshine Walkingstick," he retorted. "You haven't changed your mind about tomorrow, have you?"

"I promised I'd go, didn't I?"

"Don't mean you haven't changed your mind." He sighed and that leather creaking sound come over the line. "How was your day?"

"Oh, about the same as usual. Missy come by and

listened to me gossip about Rhapsody. How was yourn?”

“Pretty routine. A couple of people fishing in the Tallulah River without a license. They weren’t too happy with the tickets I wrote.”

“They never is,” I murmured. Hadn’t I heard enough complaints of the like from my own kin?

“Had an e-mail from the guy that tests our water,” Riley said. “He said it might be a while.”

“Wish he’d hurry.”

“It’s the government, Sunny. Nobody’s ever in a hurry.”

The slow humor in his drawl warmed me to the core. “What time you wanna step out tomorrow?”

“Depends on what you want to see.”

“I don’t rightly care. Long as it ain’t too mushy, I’m fine.”

“We’ll go to a matinee, then, right after lunch.”

“Want me to come out to your place?”

“Forget it. I’m picking you up, treating you like a queen, and stealing a kiss at the end of the night.”

“Hunh.” I bit the inside of my cheek, holding back that stupid grin. “Sounds like you got it all worked out.”

He was quiet for a long time. “Yeah, I guess I have.”

Was that a thread of regret in his voice, maybe doubt? I clutched my phone and swallowed down the disappointment. Well, it’d been nice thinking about being on a real date, anyhow. Too bad he changed his mind, and quicker’n greased lightning, too. Wasn’t that just like a man?

“It’s ok, Riley.”

“It is?” he asked softly.

“Yeah. Um, listen, I gotta go now. You take care.”

“Wait, Sunny, what...”

I hung up and dropped my phone on top of my desk, and stared at the cold plate of food sitting there. A nasty knot formed in my stomach, shoving out the hunger. Damn it all. Why had I let my hopes get so high? Hadn’t I learnt a million times over how it didn’t pay to dream about Riley Treadwell?

My phone beeped. I picked it up and grunted. A text from Riley. Danged if I was gonna open it. Danged if I was gonna wallow in my misery, either. I stood up, dug a quarter outta my pocket, and dropped it in the cussing jar. My phone beeped again, and I scrubbed my hands over my face. He was one persistent booger, weren't he?

I wrapped up my supper, stuck it in the fridge, and stalked outta the house. Only one cure for what ailed me, and that was a good, long visit with Henry. I stayed out there 'til dark, letting the calm of the deep wood seep into my bones and soothe away the hurt stinging my throat something fierce.

HARD BANGS on my front door woke me early the next morning, snapping me out of a deep, dreamless sleep. I stumbled outta bed cursing ever single morning person I knowed. The list was a long'un, so it took me plum from the time I yanked on pants to the time I answered the door to spread the meanness around.

I jerked open the door, ready to cuss and spit, and stopped with my mouth wide open. Old Mother stood on my porch, her black as night eyes fixed on something only she could see. Thing is, I knowed a lotta crazy people with wild eyes and a heart to match. Fame was one of 'em, my mama another, which made an odd sorta sense, seeing as how they was brother and sister.

There was one guy, though, this Army veteran what'd gone to school with me way back when. He come back from Iraq all wrong, twisted by too much blood and too many innocent folks ruined under the hammer of war. His eyes had changed, becoming a mite too much like Old Mother's, strange and cloudy. I always got the sense he was looking into death itself. Not long after, his wife found him hanging from a tree in their front yard, his sightless eyes still as crazy as they was before. God rest his soul, there was only so much a body could take before the mind snapped.

Old Mother, though, she was an odd'un. She turned up in the next holler over about the time my mama sliced up my daddy, and been there ever since. Nobody knowed where she come from, but we all knowed what she was. We didn't call her Old Mother for nothing, and sure as tootin' not 'cause of her age. Way I figured, she weren't much older'n me. It was her visions what earned her the name, them and the hoodoo she practiced for anybody what coughed up enough coin or goods in trade.

I stepped back and opened the door wide. "Come on in, Old Mother."

"Sunshine." She stepped over the stoop like it was a foot taller'n it was, her calloused, bare feet graceful as a ballerina's. "You dreamed of me."

"Respectfully, I didn't dream about nothing last night." I shut the door and slumped into the chair behind my desk. This was getting to be a habit, and it weren't one I enjoyed particularly well. "You want something to drink or something? I could make some coffee."

"You dreamed of the water, and the water is more important." She held up an ebony-skinned finger, her smooth face expressionless. "The water comes for you, Sunshine. It wouldn't do to give in to it."

A chill shivered down my spine. I curled my arms around my scrawny chest and hunched into myself. "I ain't got no intention of going near the water, Old Mother."

"Has the water not called you? Have you not been selected by him?"

I frowned. "I got a potential job out on Lake Burton. Ain't decided what to do about it yet, though."

Her nostrils flared. "You lie. The sun has persuaded you."

"I got no idea what you're talking about. What sun?"

"The one making his way to you as we speak." She tilted her head, listening to the beyond, for all I knowed. "Be wary of the water, Sunshine, and dream no more."

"I told you, I didn't dream about nothing."

"The water comes. It burns and seethes and roils in the deep over the old man's home." Her eyes rolled back, showing the whites, and she rocked back and forth in the chair. "The water holds death for the mother of the spirit. It demands, and the light will give."

"Okey dokey, then."

I stood and clapped my hands together one time. Old Mother went rigid in her chair and focused them eerie eyes on me. Without another word, she rose and left, gliding out my front door like we hadn't just been talking portents and signs. I dropped back into my chair on a hefty sigh. She drug me outta bed, rousing me early enough for me to forget my vow to quit cussing, and all I had to show for it was a headache and the faint aroma of burnt sage lingering around her chair.

I counted up the cuss words I used up that morning and dropped a like amount of quarters in my cussing jar, then slipped into the shower and let the hot water pound the megrims away. Somebody knocked on my door as I was stepping out, and I grimaced. What was this, the Grand Central Terminal? I glanced at the digital numbers on my alarm clock and did a double take. Twelve thirty. That couldn't be right. Old Mother'd been here not half an hour before, and she woke me up at six on the dot.

The door banged again, interrupting my musings.

"I'm coming," I hollered, and wrapped a towel around myself. I scurried through the trailer and yanked the door open, and for the second time that day, gaped at my visitor.

Riley stood on the other side, all six foot something of him, wearing a khaki colored button-down shirt tucked into good jeans. Them hazel eyes of his slid down my near naked form and a slow smile spread across his face. "I guess you're not ready yet."

I hid behind the door and peeked out around it. "Ready for what?"

"Our date." He tapped the face of his watch. "I told you I'd be here right after lunch."

I rubbed my eyes hard and near about lost my grip on the towel. "You acted like you didn't wanna go no more, so I figured I'd putter around the house or something."

"I never," he said flatly. "Guess that explains why you hung up on me."

"It was time for me to go," I said tartly. The wind blew through the door, raising goose bumps along my skin as it went. "Since you're here, you might as well come in."

He slid inside through the narrow gap I'd left and shut the door. I turned on my heel and stalked into my bedroom. Lord have mercy, I weren't in no mood for fickle men, but there I was, stuck with one. I rummaged through my dresser drawers, gathering together clothes, and slapped them onto the top of my dresser.

"A nice t-shirt, Sunny."

I yelped and whirled around. Riley was leaning against the doorframe, his arms crossed over his chest, that slow smile still on his face.

"What're you doing in my bedroom?"

"Followed you in." He lifted one well-formed shoulder in a brief shrug. "Figured we could talk while you get dressed."

"You figured... Ooo. You turn around right this instance, Riley Treadwell."

He rolled his eyes and turned around, leaning against the doorframe in the exact same position with his back to me. "Happy?"

I snorted and let the towel drop, then shimmied into underpants. "Not by a long shot. Next person banging on my door before the sun's good and up is gonna get more'n an earful from me."

"It's after noon, Sunny." He sighed and shifted into a wide-legged stance. "Who drew the hex signs on your door?"

I bobbled my shirt and gaped at him. "What hex signs?"

"About a dozen of 'em, all up and down the door." He half-turned toward me. "You didn't see 'em?"

"I was kinda busy holding my towel in place."

"You could've let go. I wouldn't have looked."

"Lying on a Sunday earns you double time in Hell."

He snickered. "God, Sunny, where do you come up with that shit?"

Since I made that'un up on the spot, I changed the subject. "What're you doing here anyhow?"

"We have a date," he said, and his voice was so calm and even, it shamed me. "Are you putting on a nice t-shirt?"

I held the one in my hand up, then shoved it back into my drawer and selected one without any holes worn through the fabric. "I ain't even had lunch yet."

"So I'll feed you twice. You owe me two meals anyway."

"And you're gonna use 'em both up today?" I finished dressing and sat down on the edge of the bed with socks, boots, and Daddy's holstered knife filling my hands. "You can turn around now."

He did, resettling himself with his hands on his hips. "Well, damn. I missed all the good stuff."

"Not likely. Who says I'm gonna go with you?"

"That t-shirt." He sat down next to me and bumped his shoulder into mine. "Can you do me a favor?"

"Maybe."

"Stop jumping to conclusions about me. I don't know where you got the idea I didn't want to go out with you, especially when I've been hounding you for a date for a solid two weeks now, longer if you count the times I asked you out in high school."

I fixed my attention on my boots, tying 'em up tight over the knife strapped to my ankle, leaving the hilt free. High school weren't something I liked to dwell on, if I could help it. "You never asked me out back then."

"Jesus, Sunny." He propped his elbows on his thighs and dropped his head into his palms. "Ok, look. Forget the past.

We've got a chance here to be friends again, the way we used to be. Don't you want that?"

Maybe I did, more'n I thought, and maybe I was just tired of being hurt. "You wanna be friends?"

"I want to start with friendship," he corrected, gentle as a lamb. "What's wrong with that?"

Ever thing, far as I could tell, and nothing a'tall. "I reckon friends is ok."

"That's my girl." He tugged on the wet strands of my hair and smacked a kiss to my temple. "Finish getting dressed. If we hurry, we still have time to make the early matinee."

"I gotta eat."

"We'll stop by a drive-thru, pick up some burgers." I pulled a sour face at him, and he grinned. "Hey, nothing but the best for you, Sunshine."

"I'm gonna hold you to that," I grumbled, but once I was in the bathroom with the door firmly shut on him, I grinned at my reflection in the mirror. I was going on a date with Riley Treadwell, captain of the high school football team, all star basketball player, and military hero. The teenager in me was thrilled no end, but it was the woman I saw staring back at me, her dark eyes sparkling, her skin flushed pink, and it was the woman wanting him to soothe the hurts the teenager had endured for lack of him in her life.

I combed out my hair, toweled most of the moisture out of it, and twisted it into a simple braid. One day, I was gonna have to face the truth about Riley hidden deep inside myself, but not today. I brushed my teeth, slapped on some moisturizer, and walked outta the bathroom, leaving that hurt teenager behind once and for all.

10

My date with Riley went fine, and that shoulda been a warning to me.

He fed me twice, just like he promised, carried me to a movie what weren't a bit mushy, and brung me home again. His goodnight kiss was sweet and tender and, somehow, even better'n the first'un. I didn't dwell too long on why that might be. Way I figured it, the more I thought about having Riley Treadwell's mouth on mine, the more I'd want it, and the more I wanted his kiss, the more I'd want him to do other things.

I didn't rightly intend on becoming his next ex. Friends was safe enough, goodnight kisses aside, and about all I could handle anyhow.

When I come home, I didn't even think on messing with them hex signs. Old Mother put 'em there for a reason, and it'd be better all the way around if I just let 'em be.

Next day, I lit out searching for Missy's ring, hitting Ingles and ever pawn shop in Clayton again, then spreading out to the surrounding towns. I even drove up to Franklin and down to Clarkesville, and no luck in either direction. Maybe somebody was holding on to it, but why? They give it back and Fame wouldn't do more'n give 'em a good talking to, but if they held on to it and Fame found out? Well, I wouldn't wanna be standing in their shoes when he come a-knocking. My uncle took the eye for an eye part of the Good Book a mite too serious.

On the way back home, I pulled over in the old shirt factory's parking lot and considered my options. North and south had been a bust. East and west was the next logical step. West was ok. Hiawassee and Blairsville wouldn't take long to hit, even if I added Hayesville and Murphy to my route. The four towns wasn't all that far apart and folks in that area tended to move around a lot between 'em. They wasn't far from home, neither, so it'd be an easy trip.

Eastbound was a sight more problematic. Wasn't nothing in Long Creek, but to be thorough, I'd have to hit Mountain Rest, if there was even anything open. Walhalla and Westminster, too, and Lord only knowed what other bitty towns. I weren't nearly as familiar with that area as I was with the western towns, so it'd probably take a whole day to scout and scour pawn shops and the like.

I checked the time on my phone. It was after lunch. Chances was good I could make a thorough run of the western towns in one afternoon. I pursed my lips and tapped my fingers in time to the Rolling Stones. Westward it was, then. I could hit the towns past Rabun County's eastern border the next day unless something more urgent come up.

I put the IROC in gear and drove through the shirt factory's parking lot toward Old 441. Hadn't made it far when my phone rung. I eased to the side of the lot, checked the caller, and answered it.

"Sunny, thank God," David said. A fine thread of

tension run through his cultured voice. "I just saw something in the water, something... God, I must be crazy."

He hadn't struck me that way, not one bit. "You ok? I mean, you ain't hurt or nothing, are you?"

"No, I'm fine." A long, shaky sigh filtered through the line. "It rattled me. I'm not much of a country boy."

"I'da never guessed," I said, mild enough to hide the sarcasm. "I was heading that way. You want, I can stop by, maybe take a look-see."

"Yes, *please.* Gregory's already back in Atlanta."

"You call him yet?"

"I left a message. He's in a meeting."

"And then you called me."

"Of course, darling girl. You're our investigator, aren't you?"

How come ever body assumed I was looking into the Greenwood Five's problems when I hadn't officially been hired? "What's me investigating got to do with anything?"

"We've had some more damage to our dock. I happened to notice it when I came outside to eat lunch, and that's when I saw...whatever it was I saw."

Lunch. Dagnabbit, I knowed I forgot something. "I'll be there quick as I can. Don't go near the water again, you hear?"

"No chance of that, Sunshine."

We said our goodbyes, and I hung up. What'd Old Mother said? It took me a minute to pull the conversation outta my noggin, which is what she got for waking me up so dadgum early. *Be wary of the water,* she said, and a whole lotta other hooha besides. Something about the water coming for me and death.

My skin tightened and the air inside the car seemed to cool. I shivered and shoved Old Mother outta my head. I could be wary of the water and still help David out. I was gonna need my camera, though, maybe a notebook and pen, too, and I needed food in my belly. I shifted into gear and pulled outta the parking lot. Home first, then David. Missy's ring'd have to wait 'til another day.

AN HOUR AND A HALF LATER, I inched the IROC into the tiny parking area outside David and Gregory's lakeside home, right next to Riley's work truck. My heart flipped over and butterflies danced in my stomach, and I scowled. One date and already I was acting like a schoolgirl with a crush.

I gathered my investigating tools together and picked my way to the front door through a tangle of carefully maintained greenery. Unlike the other yards in the area, this'un seemed natural, livable, and I even recognized a few of the plants. Rosemary, oregano, and some other stuff what looked suspiciously like herbs of one sort or another.

David met me at the door wearing a pair of low-slung, khaki cargo shorts and not a thing besides. He leaned close and kissed my cheek, and his aftershave drifted to me, something with just the right mix of spice and tang. "Hello, darling. Thank you for coming so quickly."

"Said I would, didn't I?" I tightened my grip on my tools, keeping my hands right where they was, well away from the lean muscles of David's torso. He mighta been gay, but him half naked was worthy of a little drool. "You wanna tell me what this is about now?"

His lips thinned and the lines deepened around his mouth, and for a minute, he looked near about forty, not the early thirties I pegged his age at on the night we met. "Riley's down at the dock. I made him wait so I could tell you both at the same time."

"Heaven forbid he be left outta the loop," I said drily.

The tension in David's expression eased. He grinned and draped an arm around my waist. "He's here on official business. Apparently, the waterways in this area fall under his purview."

I shoulda knowed that and coulda smacked myself for

not having it in my noggin. Maybe if I'da spent less time running from Riley and more time paying attention, David wouldn'ta caught me by surprise. I hated being taken by surprise. It was right up there with nails scraping down a chalkboard, far as I was concerned.

"We better get down there before he takes a notion to jump into the water."

A mild shudder run through David's body into mine. "I don't know if I can ever go in the lake again."

"Can't have that."

His gaze sharpened on me. "Is that a mocking tone I hear?"

"Not a'tall," I said mildly. "I was just thinking how you might look in swimming trunks, and how it'd be a shame not to see you all wet in 'em."

That slow smile of his curved his mouth, spreading humor right up into his eyes. "Why, Sunny, are you flirting with me?"

I shook my head sharp like. "Just telling you the God's honest truth, Mr. David. You got some mighty fine stems under them shorts. I reckon Mr. Gregory better appreciate 'em or some other man is gonna snap you up."

"Some other man..." David huffed out a laugh and nudged me forward. "God, Sunny. What am I going to do with you?"

"Not a thing, just like ever other man I know," I said, real cheerful like, and he laughed and tweaked my nose and called me adorable, like I was a puppy he rescued from the pound.

On the way to the dock, David give me a mini-tour of his house. He inherited it from his grandpappy on his mama's side when the old man died a decade before. Heart attack, very sudden. David's voice deepened into sadness when he talked about his grandpappy, and I gathered they was close.

After that, David remodeled the house a little at a time, the outside first. He had the walls between the outdated kitchen, the tiny dining room, and the living room tore down, making one great room what was, as he put it, better for entertaining.

Why a body'd want enough folks around to entertain was beyond me, but it was his house and he done a good job on it, so who was I to argue?

He gestured down a short hallway toward the master suite, two guest bedrooms, and stairs leading to an attic. "We converted the attic into a library. Gregory works up there when he gets tired of the city."

I followed him onto the deck and down the stairs winding toward the water. "You don't, ah, work?"

He peered over his shoulder. "If you want to know where I get my money from, just ask. I'm not shy about it."

Heat rushed through the skin over my cheeks and I glanced away. "I was curious, is all. You know, about where you work. I weren't asking about no money."

"Hmm. You know, that's the first time I've ever believed a woman who told me that, or a man either." He shook his head and stepped lightly down the stairs, one hand on the railing. "I have a feeling I can always trust you to be honest with me."

My jaw dropped open. I snapped it shut and bounced down the steps behind him, my boots a mite louder on the wooden slats than his bare feet. "I got no call to lie, Mr. David."

He jerked around so fast I nearly run into him. "Is there anything I can do to persuade you to call me David, just David. No mister, no hesitation, no sweet blush."

I run my thumb over the edge of my camera and shifted my weight from one foot to the other. "I was raised to be respectful. Don't rightly reckon I know you well enough to call you by your Christian name."

"I'm giving you permission," he said evenly. "God, Sunny. Every time you call me mister, I feel like an old man. I'm not that much older than you."

"Didn't think you was," I grumbled. "You know, for a gay guy, you act an awful lot like a regular guy."

He huffed out a sigh and turned around, resuming his steady progress toward the water and Riley, who stood with his back to us looking out over the lake just in front of the attached boathouse. "A man is a man, Sunny, gay or not."

Well, there I'd gone and stuck my foot in it again, twice in less than a week, and both with the same man. "I didn't mean no offense."

"None taken, darling girl. This is all part and parcel of our getting to know one another."

"If you say so."

Riley turned around and stalked toward us, his eyes hot under furrowed eyebrows. "Sunny."

His voice was mild for all the heat shooting away from him. I stepped onto the dock and met his gaze head on. "Hey, Riley. David was just telling me the history of the house."

"Is that so."

He stuck his hands on his hips and turned that hot glare on David. His mouth thinned, and for a minute, I thought he was gonna say something. What, I had no idea. Riley had a temper, sure he did, but I never seen him get het up so easy before.

David arched a single eyebrow. "What do you think about the dock?"

"I think you've pissed somebody off." Riley crossed his arms over his chest and glared at David. "Say, a jealous boyfriend."

I snickered. "Oh, come on, Riley. David's a flirt, sure, but he don't strike me as the poaching type."

"Fat lot you know," Riley muttered.

"I haven't poached on anyone," David said, even as a level. "The dock?"

Riley sighed and run a rough hand down his face. "Whatever's doing the damage, there's a lot of force behind it. One of your pilings is busted, same as Belinda's, almost like it was rammed by something."

"Too deep for a boat," I said.

Riley nodded. "The ones used here, anyway. Those would do damage closer to the surface of the water. This is deeper."

"Not so deep we can't see it." David pointed to the dent in a nearby boathouse, on the property of one of the cove's other residents. "Maybe deliberately so."

"A message," Riley said, and David shrugged.

"But who'd do that?" I asked. "And why y'all?"

"A bad business deal? A prank? Systematic harassment?" Riley yanked his hat off and stared out over the water sparkling under the sun's rays. "What I can't figure out is how it was done. Somebody would've heard a motor big enough to do that kind of damage, whether it was ramming the dock or had a rope tied around it and was pulling."

"Most of the houses are vacant during the week," David pointed out. "Gregory and Faith work out of town, Hal's on vacation. Thaddeus died and Phillip is more concerned with keeping his father's company afloat than with tending to his father's estate."

"The Arrowoods live here year round," I pointed out, "but Belinda and Tom work in town and his kids are in school all day."

David slid a sly glance toward me. "Not all the time."

"Cutting class, huh?" I shook my head. Kids didn't never appreciate an education 'til the opportunity passed 'em by. "I'll try to run 'em down and talk to 'em. Maybe they seen something."

"Speaking of seeing something." David pointed to the newest damage to his dock. "That's where I was when I saw a large shadow under the water."

I snickered. "A shadow spooked you that much? City boy."

"It wasn't the shadow that spooked me, Sunny. It was the

eye, nearly as big as my palm. One minute it was there and the next it was gone.”

“Hunh.” Riley slapped his cap on and adjusted it over his red-brown hair. “Was the eye attached to something or was it just floating?”

“Attached, definitely.” David exhaled a shaky breath. “It blinked at me.”

“Close to the surface?”

“Best guess? A lot deeper.” David rubbed a hand over his nape. “At least a couple of feet below that crack in the piling, down where the water gets murky.”

“And you still made out an eye?” I shoved my camera into my back pocket and handed him my notebook and pen. “Draw it for me, ever thing you remember, ok?”

“Sure.” He settled on the lowest stair step, opened the notebook to a clean page, and laid it across his knee. “Has anyone officially hired you yet?”

Riley snorted. “Yeah, good luck with that. Belinda offered.”

I scowled and put my back to him. “Belinda can go suck an egg, far as I’m concerned.”

David glanced up from his drawing, his hand stilled in mid-stroke. “Bad blood?”

“Bad ever thing.” An understatement if ever there was one. “I ain’t gonna let one of y’all pay for the investigating of a whole party. Ever body chips in or nobody gets nothing, you hear?”

“I’ll take care of it. If you’d prefer, I can be your liaison for the group. I’m here most of the time anyway.”

“Forget it,” Riley said flatly.

I whirled on him. “Butt out, Ranger Rick. You drug me into this mess, and now, I’m gonna handle it the way I want to.”

Riley whipped his hat off and slapped it against his thigh. “Damn it, Sunny. He’s trying to get into your pants.”

I threw my head back and laughed so hard, my eyes

watered. My breath wheezed out and I doubled over, bracing my hands on my knees.

"Laugh it up, Sunshine," he muttered, and slipped his cap back on. "See if I'm wrong."

"Not entirely." David padded toward us, his footsteps near silent. He laid a hand on my back, patting me softly. "I have every intention of getting you out of those pants and into a bathing suit before the air's too cold to go on a boat ride."

I sucked in a breath with the last of my laughter and pushed myself upright. "See? He ain't up to no good, Riley. Honest to God, you're as bad as Fame."

"Fame?" David asked.

"My uncle, Fame Carson."

His eyes widened. "You're Fame Carson's niece?"

"Ever body knows that, David. No call to act surprised."

I took the notebook from his limp fingers and eyed the drawing. He done a good job on it, filling in details most people woulda missed, like the odd-shaped iris and pupil. Whatever it was, it weren't human, and that's all I knowed.

I passed the drawing off to Riley and eyed David. His skin was ten shades pastier than it was a minute ago. "You ok?"

"You're Fame Carson's niece." He staggered to the steps and dropped like a stone onto the bottom tread. "Holy shit."

"He ain't got that bad a reputation." I jerked my chin at Riley. "What d'you think?"

"I think I need to think about it." He waggled the notebook. "Mind if I take this back to the office and make a copy?"

"Make a couple. We'll show 'em around." I stabbed my thumb over my shoulder at David. "Let me get him inside. He's liable to pass out on us, now that he knows my upstanding lineage."

Riley's lips twitched. "Wait until he finds out about your mama."

"Why, that orta send him running right back to the city,"

I said drily. "You reckon I orta tell him why folks really hire me?"

"I can still hear the two of you," David said. "And yes, I want to know every single detail."

I rolled my eyes. "Uh-huh. You seen enough, Riley?"

"More than, though what's there isn't enough to track down what's doing this." He stepped closer and skimmed the backs of his fingers along my cheek. "Can I call you tonight?"

"Yeah." I bit my lower lip, weighing common sense against need. One urged me to run as fast and far as I could. The other wanted me to lean into him and take ever thing he was willing to give. "You don't gotta ask ever time."

"I wanna make sure it's ok."

"It is, honest. Call me." My gaze dropped even with the base of his neck and the pulse beating there beneath his skin. "Maybe we could do something this weekend?"

"Maybe before then." He sighed and stepped back. "I need to get back to work. Walk me up?"

"Sure." I pivoted and bounded across the deck toward David. He pushed himself into a stand, and for a minute, I coulda sworn I seen something like envy on his face. "Come on, city boy. Let's get you away from the water."

"Funny."

We walked up in silence in a line, me sandwiched between David in the lead and Riley bringing up the rear. A few minutes later, the three of us were in the parking area. Riley kissed me, short and sweet, then he was gone. I pressed a hand to my tingling lips. Lord above, that boy could kiss, and I was pretty sure I was gonna let him keep on doing it.

11

David invited me to dinner, and since I was there and wanted to talk to him some more, I couldn't hardly say no. I called Missy and let her know I was gonna be out late, just in case somebody come looking for me, then settled onto a stool on the wrong side of the kitchen island, well outta his way.

I glanced at my watch. "You always start dinner at three in the afternoon?"

He grinned and opened the refrigerator door, then pulled out vegetables by the armload. "I'm working on a menu for next Friday's party."

"Not them fancy do-dads."

He laughed. "Stop trying to hide that sneer, Sunny. Your face is too expressive."

"I don't like do-dads, is all," I muttered. "What's wrong with mashed taters and beans?"

"Not a thing, darling girl." He bumped the door with his

hip, shutting it, and set the veggies on top of the island. "Woman cannot live by starches and legumes alone. Besides, I think it's past time you broadened your horizons, don't you?"

"Ain't nothing wrong with my horizons, city boy. Why, I been all the way to Knoxville and back."

He selected a knife from a drawer and centered an artichoke on the wooden chopping block embedded in the island's countertop. "I hope you're joking."

"Wouldn't lie. Fame used to take us on long drives for no reason a'tall, so we been all over the South, up into Ohio and Pennsylvania. Never been outta the country, though, nor west of the Mississip'. What about you?"

"I've been west of the Mississippi, a long way west. I traveled for a while in my twenties, roamed all over the world."

I crossed my arms on top of the counter and rested my chin on my hands. "All over, huh. You been to Ireland?"

"A couple of times." He sliced the end off the artichoke and set it aside, then did another the same way. "It's beautiful, especially when you get out into the countryside."

We chatted for a good bit about the places he seen, Hong Kong and New Zealand and all over Europe. All the while, he maimed vegetables and I admired the quick elegance of his hands. He had a way with 'em, he did, like he spent a lotta time learning how to peel and slice and dice, and weren't afraid of doing it.

My curiosity got the better of me right about the time he wound down on Paris. "You never told me what you do for a living."

He brushed his hands off and leaned against the counter. "I don't, not much. I have investments and a trust fund. The interest off those covers my basic living expenses."

I pressed my lips together over a snide remark about his idea of basic. He might not be sensitive about money, but I sure was. It weren't the lack so much as the privacy of the matter. Haves or have nots made no difference to me. "So you don't work?"

"Nothing you'd consider work. Once or twice a month, I cater private dinners for people who can afford my asking price."

"That's how you got so good with your hands, as a chef?"

He smiled, slow and easy. "I got so good with my hands, as you put it, by using them. Practice makes perfect."

"Then you must be near sainthood."

"Believe that all you want, darling." He scooted around the island and took my hand, pulling me along behind him toward the entertainment center taking up a large chunk of one wall near the sitting area. "I need help choosing music."

"Rock," I said, and he laughed. "Seriously. Can't go wrong there."

"Most of the guests will be a bit more pretentious than you, Sunny, though I'm with you. Rock would be a helluva lot more fun." He stopped dead in his tracks. "There's an idea. Let's have a party at the end of fall. I could make a good old-fashioned gumbo. We'll have beer and all the rock you can handle and not a single fancy do-dad."

"Maybe you should run that by Gregory."

"He'll go along with it. He always does. Besides, if I didn't drag him out, he'd never socialize."

"He struck me as the shy type. Not much on partying."

"I make up for it." He snagged a remote from the coffee table, pressed a button, and something slow and jazzy filled the room. "There. What do you think?"

I tilted my head and absorbed the mellow saxophone, the shush of a cymbal. "Sounds kinda like rain."

David grinned and tugged on my hand, and I went flying into him. Our bodies bumped together and I nearly smooshed his toes trying not to bowl him over. He slid a bare arm around my waist and placed my hand over his heart, holding it there with his other hand. His cheek brushed across my temple and settled there. "That's better."

I eased away, and he pulled me right back where he wanted me, about half a foot too close. I held my hands still on his skin, one on his shoulder, the other over the steady thump of his heartbeat. "I don't let nobody hold me this tight."

"Not even Ranger Rick?"

I hid a snicker in the side of David's neck. "We're still kinda new at the whole guy-girl thing."

"Not at the friendship thing, though."

"We been friends since we was young'uns." More or less, depending on who was talking. "Why?"

"You've got that way together."

He whirled me in a small circle, and danged if I didn't go right along with him. This dancing gig was getting easier ever single time, and was pretty fun to boot.

"What kinda way?" I asked.

"Easy, familiar." His shoulder lifted under my hand, then dropped. "He's infatuated with you."

I sputtered out a laugh. "He ain't neither."

"Trust me, Sunny." David buried his face in my hair and sniffed. "This shampoo is absolutely enchanting."

"It's lemon verbena something or other. I got a year's supply of shampoo for, ah." I clapped my jaws together. Reckon David didn't need to hear as how I sliced and diced a nest of gnomes about as easy as he did them veggies he worked over. "A client. You know, in trade. I get a new one ever month. July's was this."

He sniffed again, and danged if he didn't sniff his way down to my throat. "What happened to August and September?"

"Don't use 'em up that quick." I leaned my head away. "What're you doin'?"

"Checking to see if you smell good all over, and you do."

"You want, I can probably get you some."

"I think I like it better on you." He sighed and left my neck alone, resting his cheek against my head again. "I thought you'd probably shoot me by now."

I reared back and met his gaze. "What for?"

"For taking liberties. For holding you so close and sniffing you." His hand drifted up my back and tugged on the ends of my hair. "You don't seem like the type to let a man do that."

"Not much," I admitted. "Ain't like you're gonna get outta hand or nothing. I mean, I don't gotta worry about my womanly virtue, and you ain't exactly scary."

His head dipped closer to mine, and he murmured, "You think I'm safe."

"If I didn't, sure as tootin' you woulda done lost some blood."

"Fame Carson's niece. At least you came by that honestly."

His arm tightened around my back and he pressed his lips to mine, soft and easy. His tongue flicked out, tasting me, and I stiffened. He pulled back and rested his forehead against mine. "You taste like him. Riley."

"'Course, I do." I blew out a shaky breath. "What is it with you and kisses?"

"I like kissing. Don't you?"

"Yeah, but I... No." I put a finger over his mouth, just in case he took me liking kisses the wrong way. "I ain't kissing you again, I don't care how friendly we get."

His slow smile stretched across his mouth. "Darling girl, we're just getting started."

"You're the biggest flirt I ever met." I shook my head and scratched his chest lightly. "We gonna get on with the dancing thing or what? I figure with the amount of veggies you chopped up, we need to work up an appetite, and we got things to discuss, too, like who's wandering around the lake at what hours and whatnot."

"Yes, ma'am." He eased away, his smile never fading, and grabbed the remote. "How about a little rock and roll?"

"Now you're talking, city boy," I said, and for the rest of

the afternoon, we danced our little hearts out and talked up a storm, and when supper time rolled around, he didn't serve a single fancy do-dad.

THAT WEEK passed quicker'n chicken spit in the wind. I canvassed east and west for Missy's ring and had not a dram of luck. If somebody took it, they was holding on to it mighty tight. We kept a sharp eye out in case it simply fell out while Missy was walking somewhere, but that didn't help neither. Poor thing, she weren't taking it well a'tall, and I didn't blame her none.

I had a couple of other cases come in, little piddling ones, and I dealt with 'em just as quick. An earth gnome was making mischief in old Aunt Sadie's fall garden. I give it a stern talking to and it settled down right good, though I weren't fool enough to believe that was the last I'd hear on it. Aunt Sadie promised me a rasher of bacon from the hogs she and her kin was planning on slaughtering in late fall, and I considered it a favorable trade.

The lady dog Billy Kildare's Blue Tick sniffed out dug under a fence and made a beeline for the Kildare's. I brung her back and advised the owners to find peace in knowing the two dogs was sticking close to home.

There was one case I couldn't dismiss right off, and it raised my hackles somewhat. Preacher Dryman's grandmother's pearls went missing outta the safe where he kept 'em.

He weren't my preacher. I went to the Baptist church, and he was with the Church of God. Different denominations, same holy spirit, I figured. He was a good man, though, respectful of the community, even if he weren't born into it, and far as I could tell, he never hurt a fly. His kids all lived in Atlanta's suburbs, making a better living for their own kids than what the mountains provided, and his wife died some years past. Ovarian cancer. She went quick, which was more'n could be said about most.

I nosed around the neighbors some. Not a one of 'em seen nor heard a blessed thing. That weren't unusual, seeing as how they lived more'n a quarter mile from the preacher's tidy home. I promised to dig around for him, though it made me mad having to do it. What kinda sick weirdo stole an heirloom from a preacher anyhow?

Riley had a day off on Wednesday, and somehow or other, he talked me into letting him cook supper for me. We took advantage of the late summer sun and grilled out, him searing the meat, me propped against his sliding glass door. When he moved back home, he rented an apartment in Clayton. Weren't much of a yard to speak on, but the inside was nice for all that it was as Spartan as they come. He painted the walls a warm eggshell beige and decorated the interior with a leather sofa and recliner in the living room, a four-seater wooden table in the dining room, and a massive king-sized sleigh bed in his bedroom.

I didn't look too hard on that, just in case my pea brain started getting ideas it orta not.

After supper, Riley put in a movie and we sat side by side on that leather couch of his. His arm snuck around my shoulders about half an hour in, and it felt so good, I leaned my head on that solid chest of his. It was nice to be around him again, nice to be building the friendship we growed out of in high school, and it was extra special nice kissing him goodnight when it was time to go home.

Bright and early Thursday morning, I drove into town and visited the library, and spent the whole morning digging through back issues of the *Tribune*. I found the notice of Thaddeus Oliver's death and the article describing his boating accident, and I read 'em both real careful. His death appeared to've happened exactly like Teus said. Mr. Oliver was out boating one day, slipped and hit his head on the side of the boat, and fell into the water, where he drowned. Least, that's the story the *Tribune*'s writer put forth, though I weren't betting on it being entirely correct.

I dug back a couple more years just to see what was what, and stumbled on a coupla other odd incidents. Another young girl disappeared a coupla summers back and reappeared a month later. No new tattoos was mentioned, but that didn't mean nothing. Maybe it was important and maybe it didn't have nothing to do with a thing. Only time would tell that tale.

After restacking the back issues, I borrowed a computer and hammered out something close to a résumé describing some of the tamer jobs I done here of late, along with a list of references. If that didn't do Faith Renault good, I didn't know what would. When I was done, I made a handful of copies, paid for 'em at the desk, and headed over to Injun Bob's for a nice, long chat with BobbiJean. She hadn't seen hide nor hair of Preacher Dryman's grandma's pearls, but she promised to watch what come in and out real close.

She and me eat a late lunch together, and then, since I had a coupla hours to kill, I went back to the library and pulled down old issues of *Foxfire Magazine*. They done a ton of interviews on the elder members of my family back in the magazine's heyday, and I liked reading 'em. As I was thumbing through the older issues, my eye caught on one containing a wishing well full of local legends. I pulled it down and settled into a chair, and read it straight through from cover to cover in one go, paying particular attention to the ones surrounding the lakes. Nothing really jumped out at me, not nothing probable nohow, so when it was time to go, I reshelved the magazine and walked across the street to the courthouse for the County Commissioners' meeting.

The meeting room was plum full by the time I arrived and the commissioners was already ranged out at a table near the back, talking amongst themselves under the rumble of the crowd. I spotted Riley standing to one side and squeezed through acquaintances and strangers alike to get to him.

He saw me coming and them hazel eyes of his lit with a

soft glow. Soon as I reached him, he tucked me against his side, holding me there with an arm around my back and a hand on my waist. "Didn't expect to see you here."

"I reckoned I orta come since water issues is on the agenda."

"Me and you both. You eat yet?"

"Was planning on eating a sandwich at home after."

"We can do better than that."

I cut a side-eyed glance at him. "Who said anything about we?"

"I did. Let's go to Dairy Queen. We can get burgers and ice cream cones, and sit in the pine tree. It'll be just like old times."

I snickered. "That tree's done growed up on us, Riley. Limb's too high for sitting on now."

"Then we'll sit on a picnic bench. Come on, Sunny. It'll be fun."

"Ain't you tired of eating with me yet?"

"Nope." He settled against the wall, one ankle crossed over the other, and his thumb rubbed up and down my ribs through my t-shirt. "So it's settled. We'll go to Dairy Queen and have ice cream."

I opened my mouth on a retort and didn't even get a peep out. The chairman called the meeting to order, overriding any protest I mighta made, and the crowd settled into silence. Old business was taken care of in a grinding drone of monotony. I yawned and slumped into the cradle of Riley's arm. Lordy, next time I couldn't sleep, I was gonna replay this meeting in my head. Orta put me right out.

They finally dragged around to the reason me and Riley was there. An out-of-town company recently bought one of the old industrial sites what'd gone outta business in the '90s. The building was falling down and beyond repair, but that weren't the problem. The new company, represented by one Phillip Oliver, wanted to let the waste water in the site's reservoir out into the local water system so they could fill in the hole what'd held it and build something new on top.

I zeroed in on Mr. Oliver. He was a tall, handsome man in spite of his sharp features and cold eyes, and was polished to a shine in a navy blue suit what fit him like he was born in it. I nudged Riley in the stomach and leaned in close. "That Thaddeus Oliver's git?"

Riley's mouth brushed my cheek. "Yeah, I think it is."

I nodded and swallowed, wetting my parched throat. It'd gone desert dry the minute Riley's breath touched my skin. My mind leapt to the night ahead. If I played my cards right, I bet he'd kiss me after we et them ice cream cones.

I thinned my lips, hiding a grin, and concentrated on Oliver Junior's flat voice. He had reports and charts and test results what didn't mean spit to me, but all of it pointed to the water being safe enough to release, according to him. I weren't the only one with doubts. Skeptical murmurs sprung up amongst the crowd, one or two loud enough for ever body to hear.

Seemed nobody but Mr. Oliver wanted that waste dumped into the local water supply. He didn't live here and wouldn't have to face the consequences, but we did.

The commissioners debated the matter back and forth, weighing the promise of new industry against the harm that water might do to the local environment. The crowd grew restless, but there weren't nothing we could do. The chairman refused to open discussion to the public, more fool him. I reckoned he musta wanted folks showing up on his doorstep at all hours over the next few weeks, complaining about the meeting. After more'n half an hour mulling it over, the commissioners tabled the matter and promised to have an open period for local input before a decision was made.

They said something else about hiring an independent water testing company and consulting the EPD, but it was nearly lost under the angry rumbles of people leaving the meeting. I didn't bother hiding my disgust neither. *Local input* only meant the commissioners was gonna do what they wanted, locals be damned. Weren't the first time they acted on the side of prospective jobs and industry to the harm of residents. It weren't like I blamed 'em or nothing. They wanted to attract honest businesses into the county same as ever body else, but was tainting our groundwater really the way to go about it?

Once outside, Riley led me through the milling crowd and introduced me to Phillip Oliver. I shook his hand, real polite like, and stuck his business card in the front pocket of my jeans. "You know anything about what's tearing up docks and such around the cove?"

His cold eyes fixed on me from a foot above my head. "I'm not around often enough to notice such activities, Ms. Walkingstick, although I appreciate your looking into it. The lake meant a lot to my father. I'd like to find out what's going on and deal with it before any further damage is done."

I walked away from that conversation with a funny tingle running down my spine. Maybe I was being paranoid or cynical or something, but it felt like Phillip Oliver knowed more'n he was letting on. Riley slid his hand into mine, distracting me from Oliver Junior. We drove to Dairy Queen in his work truck, and danged if I didn't let him talk me into climbing that tree, just like we done when we was kids.

12

I checked my mailbox on the way back home that night and discovered that week's *Tribune* folded around a handful of bills and junk mail.

Teus. Lordy. Somebody needed to catch ahold of that man and rein him in some.

Since I had it out, I read through it anyhow. Weren't nothing in it I wanted to see, about like I figured, but at least I only found one close kinfolk in the police blotter. Musta been a record.

Next day, I hightailed it out to the cove and caught Tom Arrowood's daughters hooking school. Mercedes, the eldest, answered the door. She was my height maybe and woulda been pretty 'cept for the sullen twist to her mouth. "We're not interested."

"Good thing I ain't selling nothing, then." I dug a business card outta my pocket and handed it to her.

"Sunshine Walkingstick. Your step-mom hired me to figure out what was messing with your dock."

Her deep blue eyes hardened. "I don't know anything about that."

"You sure? Way I hear tell, you and your sister spend a lotta time out here when nobody else is home. Seems like if something's going on, the two of you woulda heard it."

A soft voice hissed something sharp from behind the door and Mercedes half-turned toward it.

"That your sister?" I asked.

"No, it's the friggin' Vienna Boys Choir." Mercedes rolled her eyes. "Of course, it's my sister, you nitwit."

I narrowed my eyes at her and let her see some of the crazy. "Watch your mouth, Mercedes. I ain't above putting you in your place."

She wilted under my stare and opened the door wide. "Oh, fine. Come in and be nosey. See if I care."

She flounced off into the house, and a younger version of her stepped into my line of sight. Catarina's features were softer than her sister's and pinched into a worried scowl. She waved me in and closed the door behind me. "Sorry about that. Mercy can be a real pain, but she doesn't mean anything by it."

"Then she ortn't be rude."

"I keep telling her that, but..." Catarina inhaled a sharp breath and twisted her hands together. "Would you like something? A coke or water. I could make you some tea."

"I appreciate that. All I need is a bit of your time."

She nodded. "I've heard of you. You know, at school. Some of the kids say you've done...things."

"I done a lotta things," I agreed gently. "Most of it had to be done."

"That's what they say." Her eyes slid to where her sister had disappeared deeper into the house. "I saw something in the lake. This past summer, when we were out swimming. Mercy said I shouldn't tell, that Belinda would stick me in an institute, but now that you're here, it'll be ok, won't it?"

"How about this. You tell me what you saw and I won't tell nobody you're the one what saw it. That make you feel better?"

Her shoulders sagged and the worry melted outta her expression. "You promise?"

I crossed my finger over my heart. "You wanna pinky swear, too?"

She smiled, not a big'un, but enough of one to show off her prettiness. "It was a shadow, really big."

"Where'd you see it?"

"The middle of the cove. We were out there swimming not too far from the docks. It's still pretty shallow there." Her teeth nibbled on her lower lip and her fingers went to twisting again. "I'm not such a great swimmer, so we stick kind of close. Anyway, we were out there with some friends from school sunbathing on our floats and I was just sort of looking into the water. It passed right under me and I freaked. Mercy had to swim me back in."

"You get any idea of its size?"

She shrugged. "Maybe as big as a man but kind of wide. I don't know. I didn't get a good look."

"You didn't see no details?"

"Just the shadow." She swallowed hard and her skin went kinda pale. "I haven't been back in the water since."

"So you ain't seen nothing else."

"No, ma'am, and as far as I know, nobody else has either." She frowned and dug the toes of her bare foot into the floor behind her. "Mercy told everybody I saw a snake."

"She didn't see it?"

"If she had, she would've told me." She glanced around real quick, then lowered her voice. "Mercy might be a pain, but she's a good sister, you know?"

Sounded like she was, though I was having a hard time reconciling the smarty pants what'd met me at the door with the saint Catarina saw. I give the youngest Arrowood daughter my business card, asked her to call me if she heard anything else, and left, not one whit wiser to what was going on in the cove.

THE WEEKEND started out about like the previous one had, 'cept nobody woke me up so dang early. I shined my roost from top to bottom, caught up on laundry, then visited with Henry for a good hour on Saturday afternoon. Later, me and Riley took in a double feature at the Tiger Drive-In and settled down shoulder to shoulder on a blanket he laid over the hard packed earth beside his Range Rover.

Ever once in a while, he got up and walked around a little, stretching his legs out. He done the same thing when we went to the cinema before, just not as much. During intermission, I got up real casual like and watched him pace around. "What's wrong, Riley?"

"Nothing."

"Don't lie to me."

He heaved a sigh. "My leg bothers me sometimes. It's no big."

"Uh-huh. That's why you're walking around grimacing."

"Am not."

"Are, too." I leaned my hiney against the front bumper of his SUV. "What happened?"

"What usually happens to soldiers," he retorted. "I got hurt."

"I figured that much out myself."

"Then why did you ask?"

I eyed him for a minute, considering whether I should punch him and walk home or give him some leeway. Truth be told, I kinda liked hanging around him, and it didn't hurt me none a'tall to be nice. "If it hurts so much you turn into a snapping turtle, you reckon maybe it's a big deal?"

His lips twitched into a half smile. "Christ, Sunny. A snapping turtle? Seriously?"

"Hey, you're doing the snapping, not me." I patted the bumper beside my hip. "So your leg got hurt and now it acts up when you sit still."

He settled down next to me, his right hand rubbing hard into his thigh, high up. "It aches sometimes. Sitting in one position for a long time doesn't help."

"We coulda done something else."

"I like watching movies with you."

"Yeah, but we coulda done that at home." I crossed my arms over my chest and bumped his shoulder with mine. "You want, I could rub that for you."

His breath wheezed out in a big rush. "Jesus, Sunny."

"What? You need help, and I hate..." I snapped my jaws shut on that comment. No way was I admitting I hated seeing him hurt the way he was doing right now. He'd take my words and run with 'em, and next thing I knowed, my heart'd be broke. "How about an aspirin?"

"I'll take a muscle relaxer when I get home. That'll help."

"You sure? 'Cause I don't mind massaging your leg for you."

"That's all I'm gonna think about the rest of the night." His eyelids slid shut and his knuckles whitened. "Come on, Sunny. You gotta know why I wanna go out with you."

My heart did a funny flip in my chest and sank like a stone, and all the ugly in my life rushed into the vacuum it left behind. I told Missy they was only two things men wanted outta me, the part of me what was a stone cold killer, and the parts between my legs what made me a woman. Not a single man I ever knowed outside of family wanted me for nothing else, not friendship, not love, not nothing. Appeared Riley weren't no different. He wanted me to hunt down whatever was terrorizing the folks on Greenwood Cove and get rid of it, and now, he just admitted to wanting into my pants.

I hated being right. Lordy, did I hate being right, but I shoulda knowed, what with the kissing and hand holding and all. I guess they was still a part of me what wanted the friend he'd been when we was kids and too innocent to know a lawman's son and a killer's daughter got no business being together. I guess I'd wanted that enough to ignore ever thing else.

"Sunny, what is it, baby?"

I swallowed down the grief clogging my throat, adding it to the rough ache swelling my chest. "Nothing, Riley. I need to go to the little girl's room, is all."

I slipped away and ignored him calling after me, and kept my head turned away from folks I passed. In the bathroom, I dried my eyes and tucked the hurt away, then I stopped by the concession stand and bought a big ol' bucket of popcorn. We still had a movie to go, and I weren't so little in my heart as to deny Riley seeing a movie he picked out special. When he brung me home was soon enough to... Well, it was soon enough.

We settled down together on the blanket, the popcorn between us. Riley braced a hand behind me and leaned in close. "You know how I feel about you, Sunny."

I knowed nothing of the sort, so I stuffed popcorn into my maw and fixed my eyes on the movie flickering to life on the big screen.

"I care about you," he said.

I sucked in a breath. "Lotta men say that when it don't mean nothing."

"I'm not a lot of men."

"You got a pecker, ain'tcha?"

"That doesn't make me like other men." He skimmed a hand over my back, slow and easy and warm. "Come on, Sunny. Don't be like this."

I rounded on him and hissed, "Don't be like what, Riley? Don't be mad 'cause all you want is an easy fuck?"

His eyebrows snapped down over glittering hazel eyes. "If I wanted an easy fuck, I sure as hell wouldn't be hanging out with you. Jesus, Sunny. Half the men I know think you're a lesbian and the other half think you're frigid."

All the heat bled outta me faster'n snap, shriveling up my insides into little bits of ice, and I bowed my head. "Don't, Riley. Please."

He laughed, kinda mean and bitter. "I told myself if I gave you enough time, you'd come around. We could be friends, fall in love, make a family someday. That's never gonna happen, is it?"

The movie started in a bang of explosions and gunfights, drowning out my quiet tears. I struggled to find something in my heart, something to defend myself, some way of telling him I wanted that, too. Friendship, love, family. I'd had that with Henry, had it for such a short time. How could Riley miss how much I wanted it back?

"I've been hanging on to that dream for over a decade, Sunny."

I half-turned toward him. "You was dating Belinda Heaton back then."

"I never dated her," he said flatly. "We were at a party together. Everybody was half-lit on cheap beer and a quart of Fame's 'shine, and she kissed me. Next thing I know, she's spreading it around school that we were together and none of the girls I knew would give me the time of day anymore, including you."

I curled my knees up and crossed my arms on top. "She told me I needed to stay away from you, that I'd never be good enough for you. Reckon she musta told ever body."

"Son of a bitch."

"You know, you keep cussing like that, I'm gonna make you put quarters in my cussing jar."

"You can try, little missy." His hand slid up my back and tangled in the ends of my hair. "I'm going out with you because I like being with you. Yeah, I wanna have sex with you, eventually, when I work up the courage to ask and you decide you can trust me a little."

"It's all most men want outta me," I said, my voice small

and thin.

"Their loss. I like being with you. I like how crotchety you get and I like the way you poke at me. I like your smile and the way your eyes go hot when I'm about to kiss you, and yeah, I like your body and I wanna be with you that way. It's all kind of wrapped up together, Sunny, always has been. When you talk about touching me, that's pretty much straight where my head goes, but that doesn't mean that's all I want."

I rested my forehead on my arms. "I shouldn'ta jumped to conclusions."

"I warned you not to."

"Yeah, I know. It's just, seems like that's all men want outta me and I get plum tired of it."

"It's not like I don't understand, Sunny, but you should know I'm not like that. You should've figured that out when we were kids."

"I'm sorry I didn't." I swiped my eyes dry and shifted around on the blanket. He was watching me, his expression kinda wistful, and it twisted right into my heart. I cupped his face and kissed his mouth real soft like. "I don't wanna do-over. I don't wanna ever forget what's come before, but maybe you could forgive me for being so dadgum ornery."

"I can do that." He scooted a hand around my nape under my hair and inched me closer. "This being forgiving is hard work, though. I think maybe I need another kiss to help me along."

I laughed and touched my lips to his, and we missed about half the movie learning to forgive.

13

Once a month, whether I wanted to or not, I hopped in my daddy's IROC and drove down to the state pen down in Alto. Mama was about a decade into a double life sentence. She was lucky the judge was lenient. Otherwise, she mighta got the death penalty after what she done to my daddy and that poor ol' vacuum cleaner salesman, and I wouldn'ta got to visit her a'tall.

I rolled the windows down and turned the radio on full blast to a classic rock station out of Atlanta, and sang along to ever song I knowed. It kept my mind occupied away from the dull ache in my heart. I took a lotta flak about Mama over the years. Lotta people told me how rotten she was, and it weren't too big a leap to go from her being rotten to me being rotten. Reckon ever body forgot half of me come from my daddy, and nobody talked bad about him, not a blessed soul.

Thing is, Mama weren't really that rotten. Yeah, she was

coon crazy, but she was a good mama. She loved me and she loved Henry. I sent her pictures all the time and helped him write to her, and read him the letters she writ. Life only give a young'un two grandmamas, and since Henry never knowed his daddy's mama, I figured the least I could do was let him learn mine. The day I told her about him dying, she cried right there in front of ever body, and where she at, ain't nobody wanna show no weakness. She never got to meet her only grand young'un. I kindly regretted not taking him down there after he was gone.

Water under the bridge.

I signaled for a turn and eased into the turn lane for Alto-Mud Creek Road, and my mind drifted to the Cove. Riley'd told me a man come up from the EPD, Georgia's version of the federal Environmental Protection Agency, and took samples of the water not long after we found that mess in it some two weeks back. They was supposed to be cleaning the water, too, though Riley never said if they was or not.

Hunh. I'd have to text him and ask.

A song by the very fine Steve Miller Band come on the radio and I twisted the volume higher. Me and Riley been hanging out for about two weeks, come to think on it, and pretty near the whole time, he done the buying and the fixing and the suggesting as to what we'd get into. Maybe it was time I done for him. A man like Riley'd be a real treat to do for, he was so appreciative.

Maybe I'd make him a black walnut cake. Hadn't made one in a while and I had a mess of nuts froze. The walnuts was about to fall, too, and I liked to keep fresh on hand. Making him a cake'd give me an excuse to empty out the old so I could gather some new.

The sign for the state pen loomed ahead and I pushed Riley outta my head. Mama'd scream like a scalded cat if I let his name slip. She liked him right well enough, always had, and his mama, too. It was his daddy what give Mama fits.

I sighed. Bad blood. Someday I was gonna have to tell

her. Just not yet.

I parked and dumped ever thing outta my pockets, dug my ID outta my wallet, and went in. The building was old brick and windowless, surrounded by double barbed wire fences topped with razor wire. A faint hint of body fluids underscored the antiseptic smell, and over it all was the scent of old. Old walls, old floors, old anger. Raised voices echoed, then cut off, and nobody looked up. Nobody wondered what'd gone on or why women was yelling. Ever body wore a flat, hopeless stare, the guards at check in, the visitors crowded into the waiting room, and most of all the inmates, like no matter what went on, no matter who come to see 'em, kids or grandkids or friends, despair was the only thing the women had to cling to.

I had to wait my turn and finally was let in to the partitioned visitor's room. Mama sat down on the other side of the divider wearing a standard issue tan baggy jumpsuit. Her blonde hair was stringy and lank, and hung down the sides of her thin face, as flat and lifeless as her stare. She hesitated a minute, then picked up the receiver. I picked mine up, too, and tried real hard to swallow down the misery clogging my throat. It was hard seeing her in here, hard even though she murdered my daddy. She was still my mama, and I still loved her.

"Sunshine, honey."

Mama's words petered out, about like they done since Henry died. Two words and she was empty. Sometimes felt like that's all she had to say to me anymore.

I tucked the twinge of hurt away and faced her square like. "Mama. You doin' ok?"

"About like always." She sucked in a ragged breath and her eyes went soft. "How's Fame and his young'uns?"

"Same ol'."

"And Missy?"

One corner of my mouth turned down before I could stop it. "Somebody stole her ring. You know, that fancy'un she wears around her neck?"

Mama nodded slowly. "I never seen it, but she told me about it once. You lookin' for it?"

"Yeah."

Or trying, anyhow. Sooner or later, a ring like that had to turn up, didn't it? And when it did, I'd be there to claim it on Missy's behalf.

I spent a few minutes filling her in on gossip, and a few more answering what I knowed about the folks she inquired after. Some of her kin and such. She used to take the paper, but that was before Henry passed on. Since then, her interest in the goings on kindly dwindled.

When we run outta gossip, her eyes narrowed into sharp slits and she said, "Heard you was stepping out with Sheriff Treadwell's boy."

I cringed inwardly, barely kept myself from showing it on the outside. "He's helping me track down what's wrong with Fame's water, is all."

"That's not what I heard," she retorted, near about snapping out the words.

I was about to dig in and argue when somebody's high-pitched laugh cut through the stale air, halting my anger before it could take root. I let it out on a sigh. "Me and Riley been friends a long time, Mama."

Her expression softened and a small smile tilted her thin lips. "I know, baby. His mama doing good?"

"Yes'm, she is. Saw her not long back at Rhapsody."

Mama barked out a hard laugh, though her eyes stayed soft. "He drug you to that shindig, did he?"

I shrugged a shoulder, let it fall. "Easiest way I knowed to meet all the folks out on Greenwood Cove. Something's been tearing up the docks out there. Friend of Riley's lives there, asked me to help round about like."

"Belinda Arrowood?" Mama asked, and I cringed again. Hearing that ol' she-devil's name was nigh on the same as hearing nails screech down a chalkboard.

"Her and others," I said, then filled Mama in quick like on what I knowed for certain. "Anything get back to you?"

Mama shook her head and slumped back in her hard chair. "Not a thing, Sunshine. If I get word..."

"Appreciate it." I pursed my lips together real tight, studied her close again. There was bags under her eyes, black circles and lines what weren't there the last time I visited. "You sure ever thing's going ok for you?"

"As well as can be," she replied, which weren't no answer a'tall.

I let it go. She needed my help, she knowed how to reach me. "I'll put some money in your account on the way out."

We said our goodbyes, quieter now in the parting than we was in the greeting, and I left under the same weight what burdened me ever time I seen her. Weren't nothing I could do for her, not really. Coming to visit, sending the occasional letter; what was that compared to half a life missed while she was in prison and Fame raised me?

I shook the melancholy off as I climbed into Daddy's IROC. Water under the bridge. I didn't resent the lack of a mama in my life, never had, but I sure would like to never have to see her surrounded by so much dangerous hopelessness ever again.

WHEN I GOT HOME, a creamy linen envelope was sitting in my mailbox, waiting there like a snake coiled to strike. I eyed it a long, long time before slipping my fingers into the mailbox and pulling the letter out. It was heavy against my palm, cool as silk. The lettering on the front was written in cursive in an even hand using what, for the life of me, looked like the nib of a quill pen.

I glanced at the return address and grinned as my mood lightened. David, that sly dog. I'd have to get him for scaring me like that. Honestly. He had my phone number, didn't he, and lived just down the road a piece. What was wrong with calling a body?

I drove on up into the driveway, parked the IROC, and picked at the letter's seal as I let myself into the trailer, ignoring the bold as you please hex signs decorating the front door. Them things hadn't worn off under a good late summer rain. I was beginning to think they never would.

Figured that was the point. Old Mother weren't one to give anything a half measure.

The glue on the envelope finally released under my careful touch. I opened it and pulled out a matching sheet of paper folded neatly into thirds, and scanned the short letter as I jittered from foot to foot on the worn, puke green carpet.

Dearest Sunshine, it began, and my grin about stretched my face in two. *I was afraid if I didn't write, you'd conveniently forget your promise to attend my and Gregory's dinner party.*

I snorted out a half laugh. Reckon David had my number.

It's this Friday. Be there promptly at seven or I'll come hunt you down myself. Bring Ranger Rick, if you must.

My laugh turned into a guffaw. Ranger Rick. Looked like the nickname was gonna stick. Wait'll Riley heard.

But if you can bring yourself to leave him at home, it would be my pleasure to dance the night away with you. Come as you are, darling girl, and not one iota different.

He signed it, *Love, David,* and added a postscript about the late fall rock and roll party he promised to throw in my honor.

I snorted again. In my honor, my foot. What a flirt.

But in spite of all his flirting, I couldn't keep myself from carefully refolding the letter and tucking it away in my hope chest with the piddlin' pile of treasures I been collecting since Daddy give me it on my eighth birthday. Weren't much in there. A few report cards, my favorite pictures of Henry and my folks, all wearing smiles like fate weren't right around the corner just a-waiting to butt in.

And a picture of me and Riley, took by his mama not long after I saved him from that snake. I fished it out, ran the pad of one finger over the pair of us, forever after framed with our arms thrown around each other's necks and huge grins on our faces. The colors'd faded a mite over time, but Riley's hair still glowed bright under that long ago summer sun, and mine was still a rat's nest even his mama's patience weren't able to tame.

I tapped a finger to his face a final time, then tucked the picture away again, hiding it for another day's reminiscence. A soft fondness remained, lightly enclosing my heart within its gentle grasp. I shoulda knowed better'n to hold truck with Riley Treadwell, I really shoulda, but for once, I couldn't find nary a reason to chase him outta my heart.

Not a single one.

14

That week, I done another sweep of the pawn shops searching for any sign of Missy's ring and come away empty handed, again. The ring's disappearance was a real puzzler. Piece like that was unique, not something a body'd wanna hang on to for fear of being discovered. Not a local, no how. Word was out, and nobody but nobody wanted to be on Fame Carson's bad side.

That left a non-local, maybe one of them roving gangs of Irish travelers. They come through a time or two and spread mischief. Petty theft, mostly, but that was enough in a small town like Clayton. If them was the culprits, Missy's ring was long gone.

I didn't wanna have to be the one to tell her, so I kept looking, kept pestering the folks at Ingles, and told near ever body I knowed to be on the lookout.

While I was out, I dropped by the *Tribune*'s office and

changed the shipping address of my new newspaper subscription from mine to Mama's. She needed it more'n I did. 'Sides. It served Teus right for presuming to subscribe on my behalf. Maybe that'd learn him to mind his own.

Wednesday, Riley come over for supper all spiffied up in fresh washed jeans. He rapped once on the front door, hard. I hollered for him to come in, and a minute later, he was standing behind me at the stove, crowding me against the worn metal front with his hands on my hips and his mouth on my neck.

"Mmm, Sunny." His words feathered across my skin, soft as air. "You taste good enough to eat. Can I have you for dessert?"

Little prickles of heat stole down my neck and my knees went weak. I leaned into him, just a bit, but kept my words playfully sharp. "You'll make do with the one I whipped up for you, and that's that."

He laughed against my throat and dug his fingers into my hips through my jeans. "Some day, Sunny."

I didn't need to hear nothing else to understand what he was a-saying. Some day, he was gonna talk his way into my pants. I didn't know what I was gonna do then, but I figured I didn't need to yet. No need to beg another day's trouble when I had plenty on my plate today.

I swatted him away, tried not to laugh with him, and failed. There was just something about Riley Treadwell what burrowed under my skin and lived. Always had been and, I was beginning to suspect, always would be.

While I finished up supper, he dug through Daddy's records and slipped one on the turntable, and I grinned when the first song come on. Foreigner. Riley sure knowed the way to a girl's heart.

That afternoon, I done gussied up the kitchen table with an heirloom tablecloth crocheted by my great-granny during the full swing of World War II. Fame give it to me when I moved outta his house back into the trailer. A housewarming present, I guess, or maybe by that time, he lost all hope of Trey and Gentry moving out. Whatever the case, it was mine now. I hardly ever used it, what with never having nobody 'cept family over, but Riley growed up fancy thanks to the money his mama come from. Dinner with him called for a mite more than a bare, rickety metal table.

So out come Granny's tablecloth, the placemats Mama quilted when she was a young'un, and two silver candle holders Missy lent me for the occasion, placed careful like on either side of a vase of sunflowers I got at Ingles. It weren't fancy, but it'd do.

We dished up plates of fried chicken, green beans, mashed taters, biscuits, and gravy, then sat at the table, one beside t'other. Riley took a huge bite of chicken, eat straight from the bone with his fingers the way God intended fried chicken to be eat. His eyes went wide and he mmmd and said around a mouthful, "Holy cow, that's good."

Me, I was torn between chastising him for talking with his mouth full and thanking him for the compliment. But today was special, it being the first time he eat here. I didn't wanna spoil it, so I thanked him polite like and growed rather pleased over the way he dug into the meal.

I was right. He was a pleasure to do for.

After helping himself to a second plate, and it going the way of the first, Riley sat back in his chair and patted his belly. "God, Sunny, that was good. Best fried chicken I've had in a long time."

I shot him a skeptical look as I gathered our plates up and stood. "Your mama cooks a mighty fine bird, Riley Treadwell."

"She does," he agreed, "but not like this."

"You better not tell her that."

He grinned. "Do I look crazy to you?"

I snorted out a laugh. "You are hanging out with me."

He dismissed that with a wave of one hand, then got up and nudged me outta the way and washed the supper dishes up over my protests. Couldn't budge him none neither, what with him being stubborn as a mule and a good bit bigger'n me, so I fixed him a plate to take for lunch the next day while I wrapped up the leftovers and tucked 'em in the fridge.

After we set the kitchen to rights, I put on Pink Floyd's *The Dark Side of the Moon* and we settled on the lumpy sofa. Riley slumped down, slung an arm casual like across the back of it behind me, and closed his eyes. "You keep cooking like that for me, and I'm gonna get fat as a hog."

I snickered. Yeah, lean, athletic Riley getting round-bellied. That'd happen on a cold day in aitch ee double hockey sticks. "I never said I was gonna cook for you again."

"You will. Some day." He tugged gentle like on my hair, and one corner of his mouth twitched upward. "Next time, it's my turn. Steaks and baked sweet potatoes at my place, eaten in front of the TV like the patriotic Americans we are."

I turned my face into his chest, hiding a smile. "Ok."

One of his eyes popped open. "What?"

"I said *ok*."

"I thought I'd have to, I don't know. Twist your arm or something. Maybe beg a little."

I shook my head, rubbing my face against his laundry fresh t-shirt. "How's work going?"

He eyed me a minute more, then shut his eye and rested the back of his head against the couch. "Found two more dump sites this week, both in creeks feeding the Tallulah River."

The news shook me outta the post-supper, cuddle-with-Riley stupor I was sinking into. "Dang, Riley. Nobody saw who done it?"

"Not a blessed soul. Tests came back on the site me and you found. Industrial waste. Phosphates, mostly, but some other, nastier stuff, too."

I sucked in a breath. Phosphates. Weren't that the rainbow stuff Fame said he found? "Where'd it come from?"

Riley shook his head. "No idea. We're trying to trace the

drums, but somebody scrubbed the markings off them. No origin labels. Standard sized metal barrels. We may never know who dumped the waste unless we catch the culprits in the act."

I sneaked a hand off my lap and onto his belly, and rubbed. "You're gonna figure it out, Riley. I know you will."

His free hand landed on mine and held me to him. "Thanks, Sunny."

"For what?"

"For believing in me."

I didn't know what to say to that, and what did come outta my mouth nigh on embarrassed me for its lack of grace. "Oh."

We sat in silence for a few minutes, comfortable in the quiet. Riley relaxed under my hand and his breaths evened out. I was on the verge of getting a pillow for him when he spoke.

"I heard a rumor about some black walnut cake."

I tilted my head up. A half smile curved his mouth, though his eyes were closed. "Where'd you hear that from?"

"David called last night. Reminded me about the dinner party. He mentioned the cake, said I'd better save him a slice."

That fink. See if I shared recipes with him again. "You gonna go with me?"

Riley bent down and kissed my forehead, then snuggled back into the couch. "Wouldn't miss it for the world, baby."

The endearment spurred a funny little ache in my stomach, shot right into my heart, and softened me in a way I never felt with nobody 'cept Riley. I searched for something to say, some way to let him know what he done to me, but by the time I scrounged up a single word, the record ended and Riley woke up enough to get serious about that black walnut cake I made for him.

RILEY PICKED ME UP on Friday evening in his shiny clean Range Rover. He was dressed casual in a royal blue polo tucked into hip hugging jeans. Relief sighed outta me when I seen him. David told me to come as I was, true, but that was usually jeans and a t-shirt. I dug out a somewhat new long-sleeved collared shirt that morning and paired it with my nicest black jeans, and was thankful as ever thing Riley was dressed no better.

The party was in full swing by the time we got there, judging by the vehicles filling David and Gregory's driveway. The sun was an inch above the horizon, round and blood orange and hazy through an early fog, and the air held the first nip of autumn's touch. Music drifted outta the open front door into the evening, some smooth jazzy number what sounded vaguely familiar. Probably something David made me listen to when he was doing the planning.

Riley come around and helped me out, and I let him, just like I let him hold my hand during the short distance between his SUV and the house.

A woman had to live while she could, 'specially with a man like Riley in her life.

I was still smiling over that notion when we went inside. Twenty or so folks mingled in clumps around the great room, some I knowed, some I didn't. David stood behind the kitchen island, chopping knife in hand, wearing an apron over a creamy collared shirt and faded jeans. He spotted us right away and beamed a smile as he set the knife down and skirted the island.

His feet was bare as the day he was born.

I grinned. Reckon he was serious about coming as a body was, then, and good on him.

When he reached us, he smacked a kiss to my mouth. "Sunshine, you are as radiant as the sun."

I smoothed a hand over my stick straight hair, braided down my back and pinned ruthlessly in the hopes it'd behave. "Go on with you."

Riley subtly wedged himself between me and David. "Some party."

David shot a knowing grin at me and winked, the scamp. "We'll have dinner soon. Introduce Sunshine around, would you?"

And he was gone in a flash toward his station at the island among vegetables and fruits and no telling what else.

Gregory appeared in his place, three beers held in his elegant hands. He handed one to me, another to Riley, then sipped lightly from the third, his soft chocolate eyes fixed on me. "All David's talked about this week is his Sunshine."

The bottle was cold against my palm. I blushed and fidgeted with its label. "Sorry."

"He admires you," Gregory said simply, like it weren't no big deal. He leaned close and brushed a hesitant kiss across my cheek, and the scent of water rolled over me, the high tone of fresh water underscored by a whiff of the deep brine. "Thanks for helping him plan the party. Work has been hectic these last few weeks. I haven't been able to get away like I should."

I mumbled, "You're welcome," then hung back while Riley took over and the two men fell into an intricate discussion about Gregory's tax law business.

The folks gathered there was interesting enough to hold my attention 'til my muscles relaxed and I found a comfortable spot between friend and guest. Faith Renault was talking to Teus and an Asian couple I didn't know. Christian stood just behind her, his sculpted features set in an expression a hair shy of bone deep boredom. Hal Woodrow was parked in front of the makeshift bar along with a fellow a generation younger sporting the same hound dog eyes as Hal. His son, maybe?

I shook the question off and shifted my observation to another corner of the room where Phillip Oliver stood gazing mockingly around, right beside a pretty little blond what looked like she'd blow away in a stiff wind. City folk. All them women did, seemed like, was shop and exercise and spread their catty little gossip. A good meal'd go a long way toward righting their moods, but I reckoned they was too afraid of gaining weight to try it.

I run my gaze back over the crowd, mentally ticking off the guests. Hunh. That made four of the Greenwood Five. All the party lacked was—

A blur of red swirled by, and my mood twisted south as Belinda tottered across the room followed by a subdued Tom. She'd managed to wedge herself into a skintight, curve hugging, fire engine red dress what stopped a good six inches above her knees. Her hair was twisted into a blonde chignon, but what caught my eye was the gold-framed ruby gracing her left index finger, a ring I knowed like the back of my hand.

Missy's ring. Well, crap.

Molten anger swept over me and my hands tightened on the beer bottle, chilling 'em numb. That bitch stole Missy's ring. No wonder it hadn't turned up. Belinda'd probably snuck it away 'til she thought it was safe to bring out. She wouldn't care one whit what Fame'd do to her when he learnt she stole that ring, no sirree. Ms. Belinda Arrowood, née Heaton, didn't give a fig what nobody else thought, 'specially some no account, backwoods hick what run extralegal enterprises in his spare time.

She was above that sort of riffraff.

Riley's hand fell gentle on my shoulder. "You ok, Sunny?"

I nodded, my eyes glued to the woman what'd made my life miserable from day one of high school on. Some folks sat mighty high on their horses. I reckoned it was time for that'un to be knocked down, but I sure as tootin' weren't gonna do it at David's party.

Riley's gaze followed mine. He sighed, then leaned down real close and whispered, "C'mon, Sunny. You have to get over that."

I jerked away from him like he slapped me, and for a

minute, I was so spitting mad, I couldn't speak. Hot emotion roiled within me, overwhelming any thought I had for the company or the locale, or even my growing respect for the host.

And that brought me up short. David went outta his way to welcome me, in spite of who I was, in spite of what I weren't. He'd welcomed me without judgment or prejudice, and he was my friend. I didn't have so many of those. Sure couldn't afford to lose one now.

I swallowed past the raw anger choking me and managed to grit out, "I need some air."

Gregory opened his mouth and closed it on silence, but I didn't care. What was I but the niece of a drug runner and the daughter of a coon crazy killer? Manners wasn't bred into me like they was Gregory and Riley and all the other folks here, and for once, I weren't gonna try to muster any, no matter who invited me and what I thought of him.

I whirled away and left through the front door, avoiding the little clumps of polite chit chat and less polite envy, and come to a halt in the middle of the front porch. The sun had fallen while we was inside and fog had drifted down onto the lake. I sucked in fresh air in great heaves, willing the anger and hurt and resentment swirling sick and mean in my gut to stay there.

What give Riley the right to tell me how to handle Belinda? Who did he think he was anyhow, that I needed his advice?

Shame hit me with the force of a hurricane, burying ever thing else, and I scraped shaky hands over my head and down my braid. What was wrong with me? Riley'd been nothing but kind to me as long as I knowed him. He didn't deserve the blunt end of my temper, 'specially when it weren't directed at him. He weren't the cause, not even close, and I shouldn't'ta lashed out at him, even in my mind.

I heaved a sigh and dropped my head back. The sky above me was bereft of stars and moon, an empty, black sea tinged purple at the horizon above the outline of the mountains. I stared into that darkness and waited for it to swallow up my shame. I was gonna have to apologize to him, weren't no way around it. But not yet. I needed just a minute more to gather my wits and make dang sure my anger over Belinda's thievery and the past hanging between us was locked up tight.

With that in mind, I walked down the stairs toward the dock, each step slow and even. A light breeze blowed across the water, stirring the fog, and night creatures sang along the shore in time with the mournful notes of a saxophone escaping the house.

The dock rung hollow under my footsteps. I walked to the very end and stood with my arms curled around my middle and my shoulders hunched 'round my ears. Fog lay in an irregular blanket across the water sloshing against the support posts, and the scent of moisture enveloped me. From this far off, the murmur of voices and the quiet music David chose was silent, absorbed by the darkness enfolding me.

Metal clanked against metal in Gregory and David's boathouse, just to the side of the dock and up against the shore. My hands dropped, reaching automatically for the hunting knife tucked against my ankle inside my boot. I curled 'em into fists instead and laughed soft and low. It was eerie out here, was all. Nothing was on the water but me and the sleeping fishies and the frogs serenading each other.

"Sunny?"

Riley's soft call floated down to me. I turned around and glanced up. He was standing on the second landing with his fingers tucked into his jeans, his expression hidden by the night.

"You ok?" he asked.

I managed a wan smile. "Just getting some air."

"Supper's about to start."

"Ok."

He dug his hands deeper into his pockets. "You coming

in soon?"

"I need another minute."

"Sure, baby. Look." He shrugged and ran a hand over the top of his head. "I'm sorry."

I shook my head. Weren't no call for him to apologize. He hadn't done a blasted thing 'cept look out for me. I was about to tell him so when a shadow shifting behind him caught my eye. Riley's whole body jerked, then slumped. He slipped off the landing and tumbled down the stairs in front of him, and I stood stock still, too horrified to do anything but watch as he slid sideways along the wooden slats and finally landed in a heap on the third landing, just above the dock.

"Riley!" I screamed, and took a half step toward him.

A low, satisfied laugh split the night, halting me, and a woman said, "Poor Riley. Ever the white knight."

The shadow standing where Riley had started out resolved into a recognizable figure. "Belinda," I breathed a moment before something hard slapped into the back of my skull and the night swallowed me whole.

15

I woke to my clothes catching on the dock's slats. Two hard hands was hooked under my armpits and a man grunted with ever heave backward. I twisted around and slapped at him, and recognized that no account, good for nothing Harley Jimpson.

I was gonna kill Fame for ever introducing me to that man, soon as I figured out how to get outta this fix.

Belinda sauntered down the dock, her bare feet silent. One hand held a half-sized shovel against her shoulder. She clucked her tongue and shook her head, like a mother scolding a child. "This won't do, Sunny. Offerings must be willing. It's in the rules."

I dug my heels into the dock and scrambled for a hold on Harley, anything what'd get him to let me loose. My fingernails scraped against a bare hand, and he cursed long and low under his breath.

Belinda bent down in front of me. The night was dark, lit

by a fog wreathed moon and the solar lights leading up the hill to the house. I couldn't make out her face with the light behind her like that. Didn't need to. I seen that mock kind expression she fronted often enough to know it in my dreams.

"There, there, darling," she cooed. "Teus will take good care of you, once his pet has taken you."

That stopped me cold. "Teus?"

She stood up and tapped a beringed hand to her cheek. "Why, yes. He's a sea god. Quite ancient, as I understand it, and very upset with us for dumping industrial byproducts into his water. Didn't you know?"

Harley hauled me backward, and along I went, limp as a wet noodle. Maybe that blow to the head rattled my noggin, but I coulda sworn Belinda called Teus a sea god.

Missy's wan face popped into my head. "If this man is who I think he is, he's very dangerous," she'd said. I reckoned a sea god fit right well in that category, if Belinda could be believed, though how sweet Missy coulda knowed it was beyond me.

That she devil leaned down and pinched my cheek. "Little Sunshine Walkingstick, detective and paranormal expert, didn't know one of the men fawning after her was a sea god? Will wonders never cease."

Her light tone set my teeth on edge, always had. This time, though, I weren't a green kid too scared of her own shadow to stick up for herself. This time, I was a grown woman what'd sent a few dozen monsters to their graves. I weren't helpless, I weren't afraid, and I sure as hell weren't gonna let this bitch get away with bullying me no more.

"Run as fast as you can, Belinda Heaton," I hissed out. "I'm coming after you next, you and that ring you're wearing."

She stood up and laughed. The tinkling sound broke through the night, silencing the frogs and crickets in their song. "Don't be naïve, darling. Teus will never let you go. Throw her in now, Harley, and watch until the creature takes her."

She swiveled around on the ball of a bare foot and sashayed away. Beyond her, Riley's crumpled form was spotlighted in the last bit of good light along the dock. Riley, him what'd survived Afghanistan and walked away with the scars to prove it. Riley, with his bright hair and big heart, the only friend I ever had growing up.

Riley, him what'd saved me in his own way, sure as I saved him that day at the lake.

I couldn't let him down now.

Harley heaved again and blew a sharp breath between his teeth. "You sure don't look as heavy as you is, Sunshine."

I narrowed my eyes and jabbed an elbow at his shins, and grazed denim instead. "Fame'll hear about this, Harley. Mark my words."

"Fame won't hear a thing," he said, but his voice shook and trembled like a leaf on the wind.

Satisfaction filled me. Oh, yeah. Harley Jimpson was gonna get what was coming to him, by hook or by crook. I inched my hand down my thigh toward the knife strapped to my ankle. "Why're you stooping to doing Belinda's dirty work? What's in it for you?"

"Money. She pays me to do all kinds of stuff."

My hand slid a few more inches down. "Like throwing innocent women into the lake in the middle of the night?"

He grunted out a laugh and heaved me another foot along the dock. "That and taking care of some problems she got with her new business."

My hand paused on my knee as the pieces of the puzzle locked into place. "You're the one what dumped that toxic waste and ruined the water."

"Only 'cause she asked me to, her and them bigwigs. The Greenwood Five." He snorted and hauled me back. "La-ti-da folk and them high falutin' ways."

I had to agree with him, even if he was scum. Couldn't get a bead on Hal Woodrow, but Belinda and Faith and Phillip was all cut from the same greedy cloth. David and

Gregory was a different story. Not ever body in the cove was bad.

"Soon as you throw me in," I said, "I'm gonna swim outta the water and head straight for the police."

"Nope," he said, and shoved me over the end of the dock.

I sank like a stone and sucked cold, stinky water into my lungs along with air, nearly choking. Son of a gun. I hadn't realized we was so close to the edge. Don't know what I woulda done different 'cept maybe fight harder, but still. I shoulda paid better attention.

I bobbed to the surface, sank once, then popped back up and managed to stay. A strong swimmer I was not, but I could tread water with the best of 'em.

Harley was planted at the end of the dock, feet spread wide, hands on knees. "You just stay right there, little miss. Shouldn't be long now 'til that monster comes along."

Like I was really gonna hang around for a monster. "Help me out, Harley, and Fame don't need to hear word one about this."

He shook his head. "The money's too good, Sunshine, and I done give my word. 'Sides. This Teus fellow won't hurt you none. Trip down to his lair might be a little hard on ya, seeing as how it's on the lake floor, but once you get there, you'll be fine."

Fear crept along the muscles of my spine, fixing 'em in place. The lake floor? I couldn't hold my breath that long. Not many could, 'specially in the deepest parts of the lake.

And if I was gonna make a lair in Lake Burton, that's where it'd be, right where nothing and nobody never went.

Panic seized me then, fierce as the burning sun. I splashed a hand into the cooling water, shooting a spray of it along Harley's thighs. "You get me outta this water, Harley Jimpson."

Right about then, something bumped my leg. My heart clenched hard in my chest and I glanced around, searching for whatever was down there under the dark surface where light shied away.

I cursed under my breath. Belinda and Harley'd both told me there was something in the water. I knowed it from the evidence I seen with my own two eyes. I squeezed them eyes shut. *Eyes.* David seen an eye big as his palm. Belinda's step-daughter seen something, too, and here I was idling my time away in the water without my knife in hand.

Stupid, stupid.

Something bumped me again, then a giant maw clamped down on my leg and dragged me under, and danged if it didn't have ahold of the leg with the knife strapped to it.

AIR BUBBLED outta my mouth before I could clamp my lips shut and conserve it. The thing holding me swam up and I popped outta the water like a cork. I sucked in a quick breath and held it tight, and sure enough, down we went again.

No telling when I'd get another lung full. I had to have a plan, had to think of some way outta this situation. Ten to one, Riley was still on that dock. Belinda woulda stepped right over him on her way back to the party, and Harley? He'd as soon spit on a man as help him.

Couldn't count on nobody missing Riley neither, what with both of us gone. Likely anybody noticing our absence would assume we snuck off together and was making out somewhere or something. The truth was a far cry from that, but who was gonna suspect it?

No, it was up to me to get myself outta this situation and help Riley, and I had no clue what I was up against.

Only one way to tell.

I twisted around and bent double best I could against the force of the water swirling past me, then groped down my leg to the maw clamped around it. Smooth, slick, almost slimy, like a fish.

Which made perfect sense 'cept for the size. This'un had

to be big as a man to hold me like it was, maybe bigger if its speed was anything to go by. We was cutting through the water like it was hot butter, going faster'n I ever been in it or on it either one.

And only one fish fit that bill.

It swam up, bobbing me into the air. I exhaled and inhaled quick like, and was dragged back under with my mouth half open. Water filled my mouth. I spit it out through a narrow slit in my lips, then shut 'em tight, holding in what air I owned.

Back when I was researching what might be vandalizing the docks, I stumbled across the legends of Lake Burton's past. The churches left under water, a whole town of buildings buried when power meant more'n community.

But the most famous legend was of the man-sized catfish living near the dam itself. Rumors, I always thought. A fish that size woulda been seen enough for rumor to turn curiosity into truth.

What if that fish was protected, hidden away by some magic or might bigger'n what the human mind could grasp? Like, for instance, a god whose heart was created in the water.

A memory surfaced, of Teus diving into the lake without a splash. What exactly was he? Was Belinda right? Was he a sea god of old, resettled here for reasons unknown? Was I really a tribute give to placate anger over her poor treatment of the water?

I sure as tootin' didn't wanna find out.

The fish, if that's what it really was, swam up again, releasing me to the night, but this time I was ready for it. I gulped in a breath, then swung my free leg around and kicked hard as I could through the water's drag. My booted foot connected with something squishy, and the grip on my leg loosened. I yanked it outta the way, kicking as I back paddled away from the fish fast as my arms would carry me.

My daddy's hunting knife. Had to get to the knife.

Soon as I thought it, the fish snagged my foot in its

mouth and tugged me under. I squawked around yet another mouthful of water, then kicked with my other foot, hitting the fish with the toe of my boot. Crap. Couldn't get enough force behind my kicks with the water slowing me down, and the dadgum thing had my knife foot in its mouth.

That was it. I was gonna start carrying a knife on each ankle soon as I got outta this.

If I got outta this.

Riley's body laid out on the dock popped into my head, like a kick to the gut, hard and nauseating, and my heart skipped a beat. No, I *had* to get outta this come Hell or high water. Couldn't give up with Riley's life on the line.

Somewhere in the back of my mind, a tiny part of me wondered why I cared so much what happened to him, but that part was easy to ignore, what with the life or death situation we was both in.

The fish released my foot, maybe to get a better grip. I took advantage of the momentary lapse and yanked my foot free, then scrambled around my ankle for the knife.

Weren't gonna let another opportunity to grab it pass me by.

My lungs was burning, begging for air. The fish was below me, I thought, or maybe in front of me. Couldn't see it in the dark water, couldn't feel it moving. I took a chance and kicked out with both legs. Luck held. I hit it square and shot away from it, up and outta the water. Opened my mouth reflexively and gulped mist soaked air into my oxygen starved lungs. The fish bumped my feet once, twice. I sucked in a last breath and held it, then jackknifed into a dive, straight toward that last bump.

And got tangled up in its whiskers.

Fire stung random spots of bare skin. The hand I held my knife in, my belly, my face, all burned under the agonizing sting of the whiskers' venomous barbs. I bit down on my tongue, refusing to scream and risk losing my last precious few breaths of air, and lashed out with the knife.

It sunk into something, stuck, then slid free, and I lashed out again.

Missed.

The fish clamped down on my legs, both of 'em this time, giving me a firm target. I slashed downward with all my strength, aiming for where I figured the eye should be, and hit. The fish let go and tried to wiggle free, but I had him now, hooked on my knife. I angled my legs down, parallel with its body, and wrapped 'em around what I hoped was its middle. My feet didn't quite meet, as I hoped they would, so I tightened my knees and held on while I worked the knife out.

Best way to kill a fish? Cut its head off and gut it.

I was nigh on certain my knife weren't long enough for the former, but the latter? Oh, yeah. I'd be swimming in fish guts while I was a-doing. I thought about that during the two seconds it took me to work my knife free. Swimming in fish entrails weren't the most pleasant way to enjoy the lake.

I was ok with that.

The knife popped free. I positioned it in front of me and stabbed, then jammed the knife downward, cutting through flesh with each sharp slash. The fish convulsed in giant undulations, nearly unseating me. I rode it out with my legs tight around its belly and the fingers of my free hand clamped around a loose flap of its skin. And I kept cutting and kept cutting, moving my way down, shifting my grip careful like between the slowing contortions of its dying body 'til my legs slid off its tail and my knife run outta gullet to slice.

I shoved away from it and let my body's natural buoyancy carry me to the surface. Soon as I hit it, the world rushed in all at once around the harsh gasp of my breathing. Crickets and frogs chirping, a bluesy number echoing across the cove, the splash of water rippling outward around the fish's death throes, and underlying it all, the smell of the lake, like fog tinged with a hint of rotten viscera. The moon peeked outta the fog and hung now above the horizon, a blurred globe. Its thin rays scarce cut the mist drifting over the lake.

I paddled in a slow circle, searching the horizon for David's house. It was all lit up when we arrived. Not all that much time had passed, had it? I finally spotted it and groaned. So far away. Dadgum fish'd dragged me outta the cove into the middle of the lake.

No help for it. I was gonna have to swim for it.

The fish bobbed to the surface and slowly slid onto its back. I could scarce make it out, wouldn'ta been able to if it weren't so close.

I should probably haul it back with me.

The lights in David's house beckoned to me across the water. My limbs ached just from the looking, never mind the fight with the giant catfish. All that distance, and after, I still had to figure out how to get somebody to help Riley.

Screw the fish. Nobody'd believe it nohow.

I sluiced my hands through the water in front of me, doing a passable imitation of somebody what knowed how to swim. Kept my knife in one hand, though. After ever thing I been through that night, no way was I letting it go, not even to store it safe and sound in the holster still snug around my ankle.

16

By the time I reached David's dock, my energy about petered out. I hooked a sore arm around one rung of the ladder and give myself a precious few seconds to catch my breath. Dadgum fish. Why'd it have to carry me so far out anyhow?

I sucked in one last clean breath, dragged myself up the ladder. Soon as my head cleared the top, I spotted Riley lying exactly where Belinda left him, damn her self-absorbed hide.

My feet slipped on the rungs. I lost my balance and slammed into the ladder, and my chin hit the top rung, clacking my teeth together hard. Pain lanced through me, a fresh burst on top of the dulling sting delivered by the catfish's whiskers. That was gonna leave a mark, but what was one scar amongst the dozen or so already dug into flesh?

A soft groan escaped Riley, and the pain was forgotten. I forced the stiff fingers of my free hand around the ladder's rails and heaved myself outta the water onto the dock, belly first. In gravity's full grip, what little energy still enervating my limbs drained outta me. I mustered what I could and pushed myself onto my hands and knees, then hovered there, shaking like a newborn calf just getting its first taste of freedom.

Pride pricked me. Weren't gonna crawl down the dock on my hands and knees. No sirree. Sunshine Walkingstick might be no account, but she sure as tootin' weren't gonna arrive nowhere in such a humble position, no way, no how.

Getting upright weren't so easy as it shoulda been. I scraped my feet upward, managed to get both of 'em under me. Shoved hard against the dock with my hands and swayed where I stood. Dizziness assaulted me, threatening to drag me under. I shook it off and stuck my gaze to Riley, and sure thing, that was enough to slow the Earth's spin down a mite.

One foot in front of t'other. That's all I had to do.

I inhaled slow and easy, exhaled even slower, and set off, pushing ever thing else outta my mind. Right foot. Riley's hand twitched. Left foot. Had to help him. Right foot. A soft groan, but I couldn't tell if it was him or me, and was beyond caring which.

It felt like the longest walk of my life.

For some reason, my mind flashed back to that day at the lake, the first time I saw Riley laughing under the sun. His hand raised high, on its way to hitting a volleyball to a friend. That snake darting through the water toward him. Time slowed to a standstill. I was gonna be too late. That's what kept running through my head as I planted my feet against the lake's muddy bottom and shoved hard, propelling myself toward him. I was gonna be too late to stop that snake from biting him. I was gonna be too late to save him an awful world of hurt.

I reached my hand out, and for a moment, we made a fine tableau. Riley arched athletically, poised half in and half outta the water. The snake coiled to strike. And me, frantically grasping thin air.

Then my hand come down on the snake and I caught it

just behind the head, and before I knowed it, I wrung the snake's neck, Riley missed the ball and splashed down, and his mama was standing on the shore, screaming at us to get outta the water.

That's how I remembered the day I met Riley Treadwell. Saving him was the only good thing I done up 'til then, and for such a long time after, it was the only good in me I knowed. Maybe that was why I liked him so much. Maybe he reminded me of a time when I still held the potential to be more'n what I was born to.

I dropped to my knees beside him, too bone weary to cushion the fall, and stroked a gentle hand over the back of his head. The hair there was matted with blood and sticky along the gash where the shovel connected with his head, but the bleeding seemed to've stopped. Not knowing what else to do for that cut, I checked his limbs. Nothing was akimbo or outta whack, far as I could tell, but what did I know? I weren't no doctor.

But I knowed how to find one.

I glanced up the long walkway toward the house. Three long flights of steps stood between me and help. If I had my cellphone with me, I coulda called nine one one myself, but I left it in the Range Rover when we went into the party. Good thing, too, as the water woulda fried it.

Still. I sure did miss it now.

Oh, well. Nothing for it but to climb.

I hauled myself over Riley, careful not to jostle or step on him, and leaned hard against the railing. I could do this. Sure, I could. What was climbing three sets of steps compared to tracking down monsters armed with naught but Daddy's hunting knife?

I repeated that truth over and over again in my noggin as I pulled myself upward, for a while anyhow, then a light breeze blew around me, cooling the wet clothes clinging to my body and, in turn, chilling me to the bone. By the time I reached the top who knowed how long later, I was shivering hard and cussing David's granddaddy for building the house so far off the water.

The party was still in full swing, looked like. I stumbled across the porch toward the nearest entrance, the side door leading onto the back deck. David'd know what to do. He was a rock, he was. I searched for him through the crowd, looking for his mischievous smile and shining eyes.

A tinkling laugh cut through murmured conversations and my gaze zeroed in on Belinda.

The room went red. That bitch'd caused enough hurt in one lifetime to last a nation for a decade. David be damned. It was past time somebody made her pay for what she done.

I shoved my way through one cluster of people after another, ignoring shocked gazes and muted titters, and when I reached her, I grabbed her arm and yanked her around, and up my fist come, the one holding Daddy's hunting knife. I jabbed that fist hard into her pretty little nose. Her head popped back and blood spurted down her ruby red lips, and I shook out my fist, satisfied with a job well done.

Hands scrabbled along my wet clothing. I shrugged 'em off and stabbed a finger at her. "That was for clocking Riley, you heartless bitch."

She clapped her hands over her nose as tears pooled in her wide eyes. "You broke my nose."

"Oh, honey," I said, all innocent like around the mean. "I'm just getting started."

David surged through the crowd, his expression concerned more'n upset. "What are you doing, Sunny?"

I whirled on him and pointed at Belinda again. "She knocked Riley in the back of the head with a shovel."

David glanced over his shoulder at Gregory. "Call an ambulance."

The Asian woman stepped forward and caught my eye. "Where is he?"

"Why?"

"I'm a doctor. I can help."

I nodded real slow. A doctor. Good. That's what I come up here for, right? "On the dock at the bottom of the stairs."

She whirled around and quick stepped through the parting crowd like Moses and the Red Sea. Her husband and a couple of other bystanders followed along after her. Teus stood in the gap she left behind, his weird aqua eyes icy glints in his handsome face. For some reason, it fired my blood even hotter.

"You knowed, didn't you?" I asked him, accusation heavy in my water raw voice. "You knowed she was dumping industrial waste into the water."

He shrugged, casual and unconcerned. "I suspected."

"You knowed," I repeated in the sudden quiet what fell over the room. "That's why you sent it here. You knowed she was up to no good and you was punishing her for it."

"I didn't do it alone," Belinda said. Her voice was muffled behind her hands and was shed of its smarmy, holier-than-thou undertone. "We were all behind it."

All. I hefted out a sigh, and the energy anger lent trickled away, leaving me empty and too cold. "The Greenwood Five."

And that explained a lot. Phillip Oliver petitioning the County Commissioners to release treated water into the local streams. Guess he figured that'd be a hard enough sell, so they dumped the more toxic stuff where they thought nobody'd find it.

Only Belinda hired Harley Jimpson, more fool her, and he was too lazy and stupid to know good from bad. If he woulda dumped the waste on land, it woulda been a long time before it was found, but he dumped it in the water, and water always flows somewhere else.

Teus'd suspected something was wrong all along. Was that the reason them girls went missing? Did Belinda offer 'em up as sacrifices to appease him?

The color drained outta David's face. "No, Sunny. No. You know I'd never."

Gregory dropped a hand to David's shoulder. "It wasn't you, Dave-o, but I swear, when I invested in the business, I didn't know they were doing anything illegal."

"You should've known," David whispered, and I had to agree. A smart guy like Gregory knowed better'n to put his money anywhere without fully researching what the doings was first.

Outta the corner of my eye, I caught Phillip Oliver edging toward the door, one hand wrapped around his wife's elbow. I blinked, and in that momentary lapse, Teus was there, blocking the exit.

I shook my head, blinked again. Nope, I weren't imagining it. Teus'd hopped across the room in a heartbeat. He met my gaze evenly, sorta nonchalant like, and a small smile played around his lips.

Well, I'll be durned. Guess Belinda spoke the rights of him after all.

Speaking of.

I rounded on her and held out my hand, palm up. "Give me the ring."

She shook her head as she hunched away from me, her eyes wary. "I found it fair and square."

"You stole it fair and square," I retorted, "and now it's time to give it back to its rightful owner."

She shook her head again and backed up a step right into her husband. Tom looked at me over her shoulder. Sadness flicked across his expression and was gone in an instant. "Whose ring is it?"

"Missy's."

He shook his head slow and easy, for once not so sloshed reality sped by him. "I'm sorry, Sunny. Tell Fame that, will you?"

"I will," I said, gentle like. Weren't Tom's fault Belinda thieved Missy's ring, though he coulda done something to rein her in before now. "I can't go home without it. You know what'll happen if I do."

He did. It was there in his eyes, the muted fear of facing Fame's wrath, not to mention losing business the next time Trey or Gentry got caught on the wrong side of the law. Tom didn't ask. He simply reached around Belinda, grabbed her hand, and slid the ring off her finger. I took it from him when he offered, and just like that, two cases was wrapped up.

Missy'd be grateful and that was payment enough. As for the other, after what'd happened that night, and what was gonna happen when all these witnesses stepped forward and tattled on Belinda and the other members of the Greenwood Five, I didn't expect to receive a dime.

Oh, well. At least Belinda'd get what was coming to her for once.

The faint ring of sirens parted the gossip whispered behind hands. I stuck the ring in my sopping wet jeans pocket and trudged back down to the dock toward the man what still needed my help.

THE PARAMEDIC pried Daddy's knife outta my hand. My fingers was so cold and stiff, I couldn't let go on my own. I shoulda protested, but since he let me ride in the back of the ambulance with Riley, I kept my mouth shut. Weren't too hard. The paramedic threw a blanket 'round me soon as I sat down, but my clothes was still wet and a chill rattled my bones, knocking my teeth together.

David followed behind in his car, bless his heart, leaving Gregory to sort out the police and the guests still lingering in his house. I sure didn't mean to break up the party the way I done. I tried apologizing once, and David just looked at me all hollow-eyed and bleak, like he lost the best part of himself.

Seeing as how his significant other was now neck deep in legal trouble, and maybe him, too, I reckoned he had.

Not a soul populated the emergency room when we arrived save the staff nurses and a yawning doctor. I shuffled outta the way while the paramedic and an EMT unloaded

Riley, and slapped away the hands of the nurse clucking over the state I was in. I survived worse. No need for a fuss over a piddling scratch and possible hypothermia.

David come in looking about as tired as I felt. He steered me toward the waiting room, shoved me none too gentle into a chair, and plopped down beside me on a long sigh.

I matched it with one of my own. "I'm real sorry, David."

"Don't, Sunny. Just..." He wrapped an arm around my shoulders and tucked me close to him. "You didn't do anything wrong."

I huffed out a weary laugh. "You think that, me and you musta lived different nights."

"I've wanted to punch Belinda a time or two."

"She had it coming."

"Sounds like." He rubbed a hand up and down my arm through the blanket, and pecked a kiss to the top of my sopping wet head. "He'll be ok."

"I know."

A long pause followed, filled by echoing beeps and shuffling footsteps and muted voices speaking over one another in the ER.

Finally, David said, "I have just one question."

My eyelids slid closed. I turned my face into his chest and breathed him in, the faint hint of cologne and the spices he cooked with and something underneath tying it all together. "Shoot."

"What in the world were you doing in the lake at this time of night?"

It was an honest question, so I treated it as such and laid out the entire evening from the time I left the party to the time I rejoined it, not sparing a single detail of what I could remember. David hmmd and ohed and listened along, and when my words petered out, he said, "You're such a strong woman, Sunny. A good woman."

I shook my head. "Ain't nothing of the sort."

He jostled me with the hand holding my arm. "You are,

and that's the last I'll hear of it. What now?"

I had no idea and didn't rightly get a chance to form one. Riley's daddy stomped into the waiting room in his sheriff's uniform. His eyes, so very like Riley's, landed on me and anger roared outta him in an oddly clipped tone.

"What have you done to my son?"

I planted a shaky hand on David's belly and eased upright. "Belinda—"

"Don't you dare pass the blame."

David's eyebrows furrowed and he sat straight up. "Sunny didn't lay a hand on Riley."

Sheriff Treadwell's expression turned to stone. "What drugs did you give him?"

David went rigid beside me. "Now wait just a damn minute."

My hand clenched into a fist around David's shirt. "Forget it, David. The good sheriff here ain't never believed a word my family uttered."

"Fame Carson," Sheriff Treadwell spat, and I nodded, like I was agreeing. Fame Carson, indeed. Bad blood stretched between them two and always had, far as I knowed. It was high time I listened to reason and let well enough alone.

Like I had a shot at keeping Riley nohow.

Sorrow slammed into me, stealing my breath. I stood on shaky limbs and met the sheriff eye for eye. Chip, he was called, but never by me. "You take good care of Riley now, Sheriff Treadwell, you hear? Else it won't be Fame Carson coming after your carcass."

I shambled past him, ignoring the arctic chill of his stare. Only one thing kept me moving forward, a single thought circling through my mind like a buzzard hovering over road kill. I shoulda knowed I couldn't keep Riley. I shoulda knowed.

17

David found me standing in the parking lot still wrapped in the blanket the paramedic give me. He guided me gentle like to his car and drove me home, then led me inside, stripped me down, and put me under a hot shower.

I protested not a word. Just didn't have it in me right then, nor when he stripped off his own clothes and climbed in behind me, or when he took the soap and washed me from head to toe, or when he gathered me to him while silent tears poured down my face under the warming spray.

Somehow he got me out and dried me off and tucked me into bed. That part was a mite hazy in my mind. Him sitting down beside me on the bed fully clothed grabbed a bigger chunk of my attention.

"Sunny." He leaned forward and run a hand over my bone dry hair. "I have to go back home. Will you be ok?"

"Yeah," I grated out, then cleared my throat and tried

again. "Gregory needs you."

David glanced away. If he meant to spare me his sorrow, he done a poor job, but maybe like recognized like, 'specially where matters of the heart was concerned. We both suffered under that burden.

I drug a hand out from under the covers and clapped it over his knee, comforting him the way he done me. "He loves you."

"I know." David shook his head, attempted a rueful smile, let it slide away. "Call if you need me."

"No phone." It was still in Riley's Range Rover. Reckon I'd never get it back now. I tucked the burst of fresh pain away for another day when I was better able to deal with it without blubbering my fool head off. "Thank you."

"What're friends for?"

He kissed me gentle on the mouth, then stood and walked away, silent and stalwart and ever thing David weren't. Soon as the door clicked shut behind him, I closed my eyes and fell into the dreamless sleep of the broken hearted.

A WARM BODY snuggled behind me, spooning me.

"Riley?" I murmured, then my brain caught up with the previous night's events and I knowed without a doubt it weren't Riley in my bed.

I shot a sharp elbow back and connected with hard flesh. A soft male *oomph* wheezed outta the intruder and a hand scrambled along my side in a futile attempt to pin down my flailing arm.

"Sunshine!" Teus snapped.

I wiggled around and faced him in the bed. My legs brushed bare flesh and something hard what shoulda been soft, and my cheeks flushed hot. "What're you doing nekkid in my bed?"

For that matter, what was I doing nekkid in my bed? A vague memory of David sliding a t-shirt over my head surfaced, and I knowed I hadn't taken the dang thing off during a dead sleep.

Teus tucked an arm under his head and smiled, smug and knowing. "I'm here to accept tribute."

I snorted out a laugh. "Yeah, right."

"You killed my pet."

"It was trying to kill me!"

"It was delivering you to my home."

"Same thing," I muttered.

Teus shrugged a bare shoulder. The sheet covering him slithered down his side, finally halting at his elbow. "I can afford to be lenient in the matter. You did learn the identities of those polluting my river."

I arched a single eyebrow. "*Your* river?"

"The Tallulah. I won it in a card game in 1807."

"That was before Georgia was even a state."

His sigh was as long suffering as his expression. "Sunshine, love, Georgia became a state in 1788."

"Well, it was before the county was formed, leastwise." I tucked the sheet under my chin. Let him show off his skin if he wanted. I was fine all covered up. "Time to go, Teus. You found your way in. You gotta know the way out."

"Not yet." He brushed a finger down my nose and tapped it for good measure. "You belong to me now."

I shook my head. "Oh, no. I weren't a willing tribute and I ain't no virgin. Pretty sure I gotta be one or t'other to measure up."

"I can afford to be lenient," he repeated, only this time his accented voice was low and husky. He leaned forward, angling his head like he was gonna kiss me, and I scrambled away from him and outta bed, taking the sheet with me. It slid off him, revealing toned muscles under sun kissed skin and an erection the size of my forearm.

My eyes went round as dinner plates. "Holy cow, Teus. Put some dadgum clothes on."

His smile widened. "When I get what I want."

"You don't want me," I retorted. "You just want somebody."

"You need me."

I clamped my lips together. If Teus was who I thought he was, and all indications pointed in that direction, he was a deity of some sort. It never hurt to have a god on your side, 'specially with a life like the one I lived.

"I can hear your thoughts."

Ugh. A sea god what could control monsters and peek into my head? What a combination.

Teus sighed and rolled off the bed. "Very well, Sunshine. In lieu of tribute and as penalty for murdering my pet—"

I clapped a hand over my mouth, silencing a protest. Might need him someday, I reminded myself, and that was enough to hold my tongue.

"—I will accept the mark of servitude."

My hand dropped away from my mouth and I gaped at him. "What?"

"Eight marks, to be precise. I was quite fond of the catfish." He strolled around the bed and settled in front of me, then cupped his hands over my shoulders. When he spoke, his voice was softer and a mite less cavalier than I ever heard him. "The marks can be removed over time through voluntary service to me."

I eyed him warily. "What kind of service?"

"Whatever I deem appropriate. Bare your left breast."

I shook my head, protesting at last, but he ignored me and tugged the sheet down.

"This may sting a little," he said, then his mouth come down on mine and his hand covered my breast, and searing heat stung ever inch of my skin. I screamed into his kiss, high and sharp, and just like that, the pain was gone like it never was.

I jerked my head away from him, breaking the kiss, and clamped a hand around his wrist. "You better move that hand 'less you wanna lose it."

He twisted his hand around and met mine palm to palm. "I have what I need. Until we meet again, Sunshine."

His figure grew hazy. I blinked against the sudden moisture and gaped slack jawed as he morphed into a slow whirling dervish comprised, if my eyes could be believed, of mist. I blinked again and he was gone, and in his place lingered the scent of the ocean and the promise of his return.

Soon as I recovered from the manner of Teus' departure, I yanked the sheet off and sought out the bathroom mirror. Sure enough, eight swirling marks the color of Teus's eyes was etched into the skin surrounding my left nipple. I scraped a fingertip along one, testing it, and yelped as a remnant of pain pierced me.

Guess that's what I got for killing his pet.

I near about laughed, caught a glimpse of my face in the mirror, and gasped. My eyes. I squinched them closed for a minute. No. Weren't no way he coulda changed the color of my eyes, but when I opened 'em up and checked again, aqua blue stared back where once dark brown was.

I was gonna have to get my driver's license fixed. Soon as the thought popped into my noggin, I winced. Like that was the biggest problem on my plate.

A knock hit the front door. It squeaked open, then Missy's sweet voice called, "Sunny? You in there?"

Missy. Blessed relief sagged through me. Something good at last. "Be out in a jiff."

I scrambled for a t-shirt and a clean pair of jeans, and yanked 'em on one handed while the other sorted through the dirty clothes, searching for Missy's ring. Nothing wet hit my hand. My heart sank. I just found the blasted ring. Surely I hadn't lost it again already.

"When did you get new carpet?" Missy said.

I glanced down and sighed. My carpet was the same color as Teus's eyes, ocean greens twined through aqua blues.

Damn it. Was a woman's home not sacred no more?

More important, how was I gonna tell Missy I broke my word about Teus? Unintentionally, sure, but a woman's word was her bond, the foundation of her reputation. I always made good on my word to Missy, always, and now look what Teus done.

Her footsteps swished through the newly refurbished threads. A minute later, she poked her head into my bedroom, one hand raised in front of her. "You found it."

Missy's ring glittered in her outstretched palm. Oh, thank the good Lord above. David musta taken it outta my pocket at some point last night and set it out in plain sight in the living room. "Belinda Arrowood stole it."

Missy's lips pursed together into a disapproving moue. "I hope you turned her over to the police."

"Even better," I said, cheerful like. "I broke her nose right before she confessed to another crime."

"Do tell."

I laughed. "Like you ain't already heard."

"I have," she agreed, then her lighthearted tone dropped away, replaced by a concerned frown. "Your eyes."

I glanced away, shrugged. What could I tell her 'cept the truth? "Teus done it. Seems like I owe him service or something 'cause I killed his pet catfish."

She gasped and pulled me into a tight hug, and I was struck once again by her unique scent, grass and the tomb and a battle all rolled into one.

"It was self-defense," I mumbled against her shoulder.

She squeezed me tighter, stealing my breath. "Oh, Sunny. You could've been really hurt. I told you he was a dangerous man."

And boy, had I learnt that the hard way. "Ease off, Missy. You're choking the life outta me."

She let go, just enough to cup my face and tilt it toward hers. "Thank you for retrieving my ring."

I placed my hands over hers and held 'em there, grateful

for her understanding. Without Missy, Fame woulda been lost a long time ago, driven under by the coon crazy what run in our blood. And with Fame gone, no telling what woulda happened to me and Trey and Gentry. Missy saved us, about like Riley saved me.

I shrugged the hurt away. Time enough to deal with that later.

"Any time," I said.

She slipped her hands out from under mine, then pressed the ring into my palm. "Keep this close, Sunny. Not around your finger, but close."

I tugged at my hands, trying to break her grip. "C'mon, Missy. I can't take your ring."

"It's not mine any more. Remember that." She patted my hand, then let go and stepped away. "I hear a car coming up the road."

Just then, the crunch of gravel under tires filtered to me and I groaned. What now?

Missy kissed my cheek and tucked my hair behind my ears. "Come to dinner tomorrow and tell us all about last night's adventures."

"I can come tonight," I said, and she shook her head, her violet eyes dancing with laughter and love and all the good inside her.

"You're going to be busy tonight, darling."

She whirled away and was down the hallway before I could utter a word. A minute later, the front door squeaked open and her voice drifted to me, mingling with the low tones of an achingly familiar voice.

My heart clenched into a tight knot behind my sternum. Riley.

Somehow, I managed to stumble down the hallway toward him, scarce able to believe it, but there he was, tall and broad and handsome, standing in my living room looking around like he never seen the place before.

I followed his gaze and understood exactly why he might

feel that way. Ever thing was fresh and new, painted by Teus's hand in the blues and greens he favored, save for the creamy white walls. The stove and fridge was deep blue, the sofa seaweed green, but what really caught my eye was the cussing jar. It was no longer half full of quarters. Natural pearls lived there instead, a whole jar full.

A disbelieving laugh huffed outta me. Reckon the preacher man'd have a high ol' time figuring out how to convert them into cash.

"Sunny."

Riley's rich voice drew my attention back to the here and now. I stood where I was, torn between running to him and running away.

He held out a hand. "C'mere, baby."

And that settled it. I raced across the room and jumped, and he caught me to him, murmuring soft words I couldn't quite catch.

"Missed you," he said at last.

I eased away from him and placed my hands on his chest. "Sorry I couldn't be at the hospital when you woke up."

"Mom and Dad were there." He searched my gaze for a moment, then wrapped me up tight in his arms again. "Dad was ugly to you."

I mmphed out an agreement against his chest.

"I'm sorry, Sunny. He had no right."

"He loves you." I felt more than heard Riley's sigh, and added, "He does."

"I know."

We stood like that for a long time, long enough for me to absorb the smell of hospital antiseptic clinging to his skin under the mountain air scent of clothesline dried laundry.

Finally, my impatience got the better of me. "You can let go now, Riley."

His laugh was a gentle rumble under my cheek. "Not if I can help it. Brunch?"

"Your treat?"

"Better. My place."

A slow smile worked its way outta my heart onto my lips. "Lemme guess. Steak and baked sweet potatoes."

"Eggs and bacon, smart ass. We can do the steaks for supper."

And we did.

Acknowledgments

No novel is written in a vacuum, and *Greenwood Cove* is certainly not an exception to that rule. Many people had a hand in helping me turn Sunshine Walkingstick from a stray idea that popped into my head one day into a fully realized character with her own story to tell.

Richard E. Hopkins, Jr., has served as my developmental editor from the first page of my first novel until today. He's also my go-to gun expert and my in-house legal counsel, and advised me on many aspects of both throughout this book. Additionally, he helped conduct research on Georgia's Department of Natural Resources, locally known as the Squirrel Police. (Sorry, Derek.)

Jewel Suddeth served as the managing librarian of the Rabun County Public Library in Clayton, Georgia, for decades before her retirement a few years back. It is to her and her former staff that credit is due for the retention of topographical maps, the on-site collection of *Foxfire Magazine*, and other reference material used to fill in necessary details in *Greenwood Cove*.

Serenity Richards, the librarian of the Albert Carlton – Cashiers Library in Cashiers, North Carolina, and her staff helped choose *Greenwood Cove*'s first cover.

Dave Tabler maintains AppalachianHistory.net, on which he published "The Story of the Wampus Cat."

Finally, my son Caleb serves as a continual source of inspiration and feedback. Without him, I would never be able to write.

My sincere appreciation and gratitude to everyone who helped make *Greenwood Cove* possible, and to all of you for taking a chance on Sunny.

ABOUT

Celia Roman lives in the Southern Appalachians, surrounded by generations of family and myth. Her stories are inspired by a natural interest in the paranormal and too many late night reruns of *Supernatural.* Find her online at:

www.celiaroman.com

SUNSHINE WALKINGSTICK SERIES
Hunter
Greenwood Cove
The Deep Wood
Cemetery Hill
Witch Hollow
Devil's Branch
Vampire Alley

KAYA FOX SERIES
A Vision in Death

VANESSA KINLEY, WITCH PI SERIES
The Single Witch's Guide to Online Dating
Between a Witch and a Hard Place
A Witch and Her Familiar
Black Witch Rising
A Witch Called Justice

The Deep Wood
Sunshine Walkingstick, Book 2

paint·er (pānt'-ər) *n.*
Slang used in the Southern Appalachians
to describe a panther or mountain lion.

Wind whipped around me, blocked none a'tall by the man steering the motorcycle I was on. When David Eckstrom invited me out for a ride, I couldn't hardly turn him down. Me and him was friends of a sort, and my friends was few and far between.

'Course, that weren't the only reason. I was partly responsible for David's current emotional slump. A coupla weeks back, we learnt David's significant other, Gregory Hightower, fell in with a business venture led by Phillip Oliver and Belinda Arrowood, joined by Hal Woodrow and Faith Renault. Together, the Greenwood Five, so called as they all owned homes along the shores of Greenwood Cove on Lake Burton, was now under investigation for dumping industrial waste into the local streams as part of that venture.

Gregory swore up one side and down the other he knowed not one speck about them illegal activities. He was a good sort, a right stand up guy, so I believed him. David didn't, and therein lay the problem.

Couldn't argue with a broke heart. I tried cajoling instead. Weren't working, what I could tell, but I kept trying anyhow. I knowed what a broke heart felt like and I sure didn't want one of my friends falling under the same spell.

David slowed his Kawasaki KLR 650, a monster of a motorcycle. I peeked around him, sucked in a breath, and tightened my hands on his waist. The road ahead rose sharp and steep, then curved outta sight, and in between, worn ruts deeper'n the bike's tires pitted the packed dirt.

I closed my eyes tight. What'd ever possessed me to get on the back of this thing anyhow?

"Hold on, Sunshine," David said softly right in my ear, and I flinched. First time I ever wore a helmet. Took a bit of getting used to, 'specially with a mike system wired into it. Them was too fancy for me and my daddy way back when I was a kid and he used to take me out riding on the back of his old beater, a Yamaha Enduro Daddy bought off a desperate neighbor for fifty dollars and a cord of split firewood.

I smiled as memory woke. That thing was older'n me when Daddy got it, but man, did he love that bike. He tore the roads up with it, half the time with me on the back and neither of us wearing a helmet or protective gear of no kind. I smiled into the memories, of Daddy's laughter mingling with the air roaring past my ears, of burying my face in his back when I was scared and wallowing in the scent what was his alone. Laundry detergent, Old Spice, and love. That was my daddy, and about the only thing I had left of him besides his IROC and the hunting knife I wore strapped to my right ankle under the stiff leather of my boot.

The motorcycle lurched upward. I leaned forward into David and bit my tongue, holding back the curses popping into my mouth. I done give the church as much cussing money as I intended for a while. The last gallon jar full I give, the quarters, one for each dirty word, was changed to pearls by a minor deity going by the name of Abercio Okeanos, Teus to his friends. He seemed to've taken a liking to me, more's the pity. Last time we met, he left me with a redecorated home, eyes the color of the ocean, and eight marks of service circling my left nipple, each one a multi-colored swirl matching my new eyes.

My cheeks heated, and for once, I was glad of the helmet's coverage. Them marks was embarrassing. Thankfully, nobody'd seen 'em right yet, but with the rate me and Riley Treadwell was stepping out, them being discovered was just a matter of time. Him and me went way back, but it was the here and now what concerned me. What was he gonna do when he discovered them marks?

Likely have a conniption, judging by how he reacted ever time he thought another man wanted me. Which was plum ridiculous. Me and him was a-courtin', and he was as much man as I could handle. About the only one I wanted to handle, truth be told, and he knowed it.

David revved the motorcycle's engine, and we crested the hill onto a plateau. "Uh-oh," he whispered.

I peeked around his helmet and frowned. A black painter lay partway across the road, a big'un, too. I glanced up. Three turkey buzzards circled overhead, their wings spread. They'd be down here soon, pecking away like the carrion they was. Best take a quick look-see before that happened, in case that painter run afoul of something in my line of work.

Monsters made just as good food for buzzards as wildlife, and got rid of some bad in the world at the same time. Two birds, one stone. Efficient are us.

I patted David's waist and said, "We need to stop."

The motorcycle slowed immediately, gearing down in a muted roar as David eased it to a stop in front of the painter. I got off and fumbled with my helmet, and side-stepped outta the way while David slung his leg over the bike and dismounted.

"Here," he said, then his hands brushed mine away and the helmet's fastening give way under his nimble fingers.

I slid the helmet off and muttered a brief thanks, walked toward the painter and sniffed. The air was pure, tinged only by the faint odor of rotting leaves and an even fainter hint of water. A nearby creek, like as not. Water run plentiful among the rolling hills. It was the painter what was outta place. I knelt beside it and eyed the carcass. No bullet wounds, no claw marks, not on the up side nohow. The fur was unruffled and gleamed blue-black under the sunlight streaming through the autumn touched trees.

I poked gently at one massive paw with a gloved finger. It was stiff, ungiving. First frost hadn't hit yet. The nights were cool, but not yet cold. Probably hadn't died of exposure, 'less it'd got disoriented and lost its way. How could a creature of the deep wood do that, though, 'specially one as fit and, presumably, young as this'un was?

David's feet scuffed across sparse gravel through fallen leaves. He knelt beside me, pulled off a glove, and run a bare palm across the painter's fur. "Still warm."

I sat back on my haunches. Rigor mortis had set in, yet the body was still warm? The hairs on the back of my neck tingled and my shoulders hunched under the armored mesh jacket David forced on me before we set off. I weren't no mortician, but even I knowed that weren't right.

I snagged his elbow and tugged. "Don't touch it no more, ya hear?"

David withdrew his hand and rested it on his jean-clad thigh. "Foul play?"

"I don't know."

But I knowed who might. Riley worked with Georgia's Department of Natural Resources. Patterson Gap Road cut through national forest, outside of Riley's jurisdiction, but he probably played nice with the forest rangers and had contact numbers and whatnot for 'em.

I fished my cellphone out of a jacket pocket and waggled it at David. "Gimme a minute."

David tilted his head toward me and smirked. "Tell Ranger Rick I said hello."

I snorted out a laugh, then stood and paced away from

him. Riley liked David well enough, 'cept when I was around. For some reason, he had this notion planted in his head that David wanted me, which was plum crazy. David was gay. I was a woman. He was a big flirt, sure, but that was all there was to it.

Just to be on the safe side, I put another dozen feet between me and David, then punched the preset call button for Riley. Five rings later, an automated message played and I was dumped into his cellphone's voice mail. Weren't a huge surprise. It was Sunday morning. Riley'd be in church with his mama, just like he was ever Sunday morning. He tried talking me into it, but I parted ways with the Christ child when Henry died, God rest him, and ain't found my way back since.

I outlined what we found, hesitated a bit. Me and Riley been dating nigh on a month now and it was still a mite awkward, for my part anyhow. I glanced over my shoulder. David had his back to me, so I made a soft kissy noise into the phone and hung up with my cheeks flaming hot.

This dating thing was tough going sometimes.

I shoved my phone into my back jeans pocket as I shambled over to David, still crouched beside the fallen painter. "Left a message for him."

David glanced up at me, his eyes squinted against the sun hanging in a pure azure sky. "Should we move her out of the road?"

I shook my head reflexively, paused. Not a lot of traffic out here, what with the road being so bad and all, but if a Jeep or truck topped that hill near dusk, the driver might miss the painter. It was big enough to cause a vehicle to flip or otherwise do real damage.

I sighed. "Yeah, we better. I got the front paws."

David nodded and stood, and I bent over. On the way down, the painter's eyes, permanently open in death, caught my gaze and I stopped in mid-stoop. Human eyes stared back at me, deep brown, round of pupil. Eyes about like I had before that no good scoundrel Teus changed 'em blue.

Well, crap. This weren't no painter after all, not a natural one nohow, and I had no idea what to do about it.

The Deep Wood
Sunshine Walkingstick, Book 2

To learn more, visit:

www.celiaroman.com